Crushed Velvet and Cashmere 2

K.L. HALL

#BLP

This is a work of fiction. Names, characters, places, and incidents are either products of the author's imagination or used fictitiously. Any similarity to actual events or locales or persons, living or dead, is entirely coincidental.

Visit bit.ly/readBLP to join our mailing list for sneak peeks and release day links!

B. Love Publications - where Authors celebrate black men, black women, and black love.

To submit a manuscript for consideration, email your first three chapters to blovepublications@gmail.com with SUBMISSION as the subject.

The BLP Podcast – bit.ly/BLPUncovered

Let's connect on social media!

Facebook - B. Love Publications

Twitter - @blovepub

Instagram - @blovepublications

Synopsis

Kasim Barnes is the cause and the cure.

His pieces fit mine, furnishing the spaces where I am void, abundant where I am scarce.

And yet, he's everything I should *never* have wanted.

I want nothing more than to free my heart from his chains, but when he anchors his eyes on me, I forget to breathe.

I didn't know what falling for him would do to me.

That our attraction would burn so hot that it hurt.

That he would destroy me inside and out.

That finding out the truth would change *everything*.

They say all great love stories either end in happily ever after or tragedy and tears.

Well, ours may just start a war.

"It's just us against the world
When the smoke clears
All we got is all we got
It's always us, never them."
—SZA

One

JRUE

THE ORGAN in my chest quaked and then stopped beating altogether. "W–what did you say?" I stuttered, eyes pinned on Yara. I stood there praying she didn't repeat the words fiancée and getting married *this* weekend in the same sentence again.

"I said, this is Cena McQueen and her fiancé, Kasim Barnes. These two are tying the knot next weekend," she announced for the second time.

Goddammit, she did it. My cheeks burned as I tore my eyes to the floor and then pinged them around the restaurant. A couple was sitting across from each other, eating so silently they should've come alone. Another group of three friends were cackling and clinking their martini glasses together as if they didn't have a care in the world. Amid my unraveling, my heart started to beat again. My ears began hearing correctly, and I regained almost all feeling in my legs.

"N–nice to meet you," I pushed out before forcing my starved lungs to draw fresh air. I wanted to avoid speaking, out of fear that my voice would crack and crumble, but I was glad at least something came out.

"Nice to meet you too." His fiancée greeted me.

The diamond on her finger glistened with even the slightest movement, and I instantly felt sick. Sweat clung to my spine. I knew Kas was staring a hole into the side of my face, but I couldn't look at him. Not again. Not in the moment. Because if I did, I would've surely died.

"I'm sorry, but I have to go. I–I, um, left my phone in the car," I stammered before spinning on my heels.

I knew my excuse wasn't airtight, but I didn't care. I sailed through the door with my heart racing a million miles a minute. Kas's voice boomed behind me as I trekked down the sidewalk. "Jrue, wait!"

"No! Leave me alone! Leave me the fuck alone!" I hissed back, still pacing toward my car.

"Jrue, please, just let me explain everything!"

I slammed my body into my car and hurriedly started the engine. His palms collided with my window before I jerked away from the curb and sped off like a bat out of hell.

* * *

YARA MET me back at the apartment thirty minutes later, still unable to pick up her jaw. By that point, I was sitting on the couch surrounded by a mountain of wet, balled-up tissues, unable to hold in my heartbreak any longer.

"Oh my God, Jrue! Are you okay? What the fuck was that back at the restaurant?"

"I think you're gonna want to sit down."

Yara's brown eyes grew wide before she swatted a pile of tissues off the couch and took a seat. "Oh, wait. Wait a goddamn minute, bitch. Was that—"

"WorkBae? Yup," I confirmed.

"Get the fuckouttahere," she mumbled, hand clasped over her lips. "And not once did he mention being engaged or having a girl? None of that?"

"No. Nothing! Not ever! But didn't I tell you I felt like he was hiding something from me? See, I knew it in my gut the entire fucking time!"

"Ask the universe, and you shall receive, whether you're ready for it or not," she said while picking at a loose thread on the corner of the throw pillow clutched to her chest.

I watched her for a few seconds. She looked uncomfortable even though she was holding onto something soft and comfortable. "What did you need to tell me?" I quizzed.

Her dark, arched brows snapped together. "What?"

"Earlier, before all this shit happened, you told me there was something you needed to tell me. What was it?"

"Oh. That? That's nothing. It can wait."

"Are you sure?"

She bobbed her head up and down. "Yes. Positive."

"What happened after I left the restaurant?"

"Well, it was awkward. He excused himself and ran after you. I mean, you were there one minute and gone the next. I didn't know you could move that fast," Yara stated, trying to crack a small joke.

"Yeah, well, I had to get the hell out of there. I was mortified."

"And this entire time, he gave off not one clue? You were just at his place, right? No traces of another woman there?"

"What did you want me to do, go snooping through his dresser drawers and underneath his bathroom sink? I wasn't on that type of time with him, Ya-Ya. Anytime we were together, it was always about us. Me and him. And now I find out my best friend is planning his fucking wedding."

The word *wedding* fell off my tongue, triggering another round of fresh tissues and tears. My eyes were already bloodshot and puffed up like marshmallows, yet I still avoided eye contact with her. He humiliated me in front of my best friend and his wife-to-be, who I was sure looked at me as nothing but a side chick.

Yara leaned in to rub my back. "I swear to the big man above I had no clue that WorkBae was her fiancé, Jrue. If I did, I would've put you up on game!"

My chin trembled as I swiped the cotton soft tissue against my nose. "I know. I know you would've. I just can't fuckin' believe him. Like, you really can't trust anybody out here."

"I mean, I know niggas are scandalous, but wow. He's nothing but a crash mission waiting to happen, girl. I'm surprised you didn't blow up on him."

"You and me both, but I was too stuck to move. I'm surprised I got out the words I did. My throat was so tight it felt like somebody was choking the hell out of me."

"I mean, I'm glad you didn't go off. She's still my client, and that's still my job, you know? But you would've been well within your right if you did."

I shot my eyes toward her. "So you're still going to go through with it—doing the wedding? I mean, I know I can't ask you not to."

"Now that I know what I know, I swear if there were a way out of it, I would take it. I can't imagine how much this sucks for you right now. What happened on your end when he chased after you? Have you heard from him since?"

I shook my head. "Not since I blocked him. He'd been calling my phone nonstop since I left him screaming at my taillights."

Yara chuckled. "You had the man screaming in public, Jrue? What did he say?"

"He wasn't screaming, I guess. I don't know. He said something about wanting to explain, but I was done. I wanted to get the hell out of there. That's all that was on my mind," I said, wiping my cheeks every few seconds.

Just hours ago, I was dickmatized and seeing stars. And then suddenly, that all had been reduced to shit. Now, my new safe space would be old episodes of *The Golden Girls* and *Living Single*, a pack or two of Oreos, and a few boxes of tissues.

"What's the last thing he said to you?" she questioned. "Like, did you hear a piece of an explanation?"

"Why does it sound like you are going so hard for WorkBae right now?" I quizzed.

"I'm not. I'm just trying to get the whole story, girl."

I sighed before looking down at my phone to reread our last text exchange before I blocked his lying ass.

KAS: *I'm sorry I got caught up. Are you still at my spot? We need to talk.*

Me: *No. Meeting a friend for lunch. Can we meet up later?*

Kas: *Yeah.*

. . .

"HE SAID he wanted to talk. Well, that we needed to talk."

"You think he was gonna tell you today? Fine fuckin' time."

I shrugged. "I don't know. Doesn't fuckin' matter now anyway."

"Why not?"

My forehead creased. "What do you mean why not? You were there, Yara. You had a front-row seat to the most embarrassing moment of my life." I griped while tossing my hands in the air.

"I know all of that, and by no means am I excusing what he did, but I'm just saying, you're not the least bit curious about the backstory? I mean, I've been meeting with this woman for months, and not once has he dropped by. She barely brings him up."

"Is that supposed to make me feel better?"

"No. No. I'm just sayin'. If it were me, I would want to know. I'm not sayin' I'd forgive the nigga, but knowin', I don't know, I think knowin' would bring me some peace or at least a bit of closure."

My sunken shoulders lightly rose and fell. "Yeah, well, I don't know about all that. I don't know anything anymore. It's like, I can't stop these fuckin' dumb-ass flashbacks of us in my head. I–I don't know, Yara. I thought–I thought he was the—"

"Nope," she cut me off, "don't say it. Don't give him that much power. You're already heartbroken enough."

I dipped my chin. "You're right. Fuck him and his expensive ass wedding."

Yara shot both of her middle fingers in the air. "Super-*duper* fuck him."

* * *

I WOKE up on the couch, hours later, to banging on our front door. It was loud. It was crass. It was desperate. I knew it was *him.* Yara's wide eyes shot to mine as she came barreling down the hall from her bedroom. "You don't think that's him, do you?"

"Jrue?" Kas called out from the other side of the thick door. "Can we please talk?"

"Get rid of him," I ordered her while wiping my eyes. "I don't want to see his ass."

"Okay, okay. You go in the back. I'll let you know when he's gone," she assured me.

"Thanks."

I skated down the narrow hallway to my room, cracking the door halfway. Just because I didn't want to see him didn't mean I didn't want to hear their conversation. I paced back and forth, trying to decide if I was going to eavesdrop by the door or sit back against the bed. My feet stopped at the edge of the door, ears straining to listen, when I heard the front door creak open.

"Is she here?" he asked.

"She doesn't want to see you. Go home to your fiancée," Yara responded.

"Can I please talk to her? I just need a minute to explain."

The second I heard his voice, what was left of my heart crashed and burned. I leaped off the bed to close the door before pressing my back against it. *Breathe, Jrue. Just breathe*, I told myself while drawing deep breaths and exhaling through my nose. Warm tears slipped down my cheeks as I crept toward my bed. After turning on the TV, Yara knocked a few minutes later.

"Is he gone?" I inquired, raising a questioning brow.

She nodded. "Yup. He's gone."

I pulled a fresh tissue from the box on my nightstand and dabbed it against my puffy eyes before lying back down and turning the TV volume down. "Good. Thank you."

"But he did leave something for you."

"Whatever it is, just throw it away. I don't want it."

"Are you sure? I mean, sure, you're mad now, but you won't be forever," she said, waving a black box in her hand.

"I said, throw it away."

"Don't you wanna know what it is first?"

"I don't care, Ya-Ya. Just throw the shit in the fuckin' trash can, damn!" I snapped.

She pushed out a frustrated sigh. "Well," she paused, "do you mind if I see what it is first?"

"Do whatever you want. I don't care. Just close my door behind you." I turned my attention back to the TV. The minute she gasped, I snapped my eyes back to her. "What?"

"Nothing. It's nothing."

"What is it?"

"I think you should see for yourself."

"Why can't you just tell me?"

She snapped the box closed. "You know what, I'll just leave it here, and you can see what it is for yourself or toss it in the trash if that's what you really wanna do."

Yara placed Kas's gift at the foot of my bed before leaving and closing my bedroom door behind her. A few minutes after she left, I sat up and swiped up the black velvet jewelry box. My eyes rolled skyward, with my mind fully expecting to see a tennis bracelet or whatever expensive, *I'm sorry,* jewelry he decided to purchase. I cracked open the box to see a black USB drive with a small note attached that said *Play me.*

I released a stifled breath. My mind swam with thoughts on what could be on the drive before I closed the box and placed it at my bedside. I was curious, but not enough to play it. I fell back against the pillows and pulled the covers over my head. Kas had managed to drive me up a wall, around the corner, and back again. Whenever I closed my eyes, his face was there. Whenever I opened them, I thought about the box. One thing was for sure: A snake, no matter how alluring, intriguing, or exotic, was *still* a snake. And Kasim Barnes couldn't be trusted.

KAS

LETTING Jrue get away was one of the most foolish things I'd ever done. With the death of Silas McQueen, I was finally forced to stop running from the hard conversation with her, only for the shot clock to run out on a nigga anyway. Not only did Jrue find out I was getting married to another woman in one of the worst ways possible, I knew I'd probably embarrassed Cena, too, by leaving her side and chasing after another woman in public.

Defeated, I paced back toward the restaurant. Minutes later, I watched Cena step onto the sidewalk before her eyes traveled across the street and landed on mine. She waited for me to cross and get within earshot before she spoke.

"Care to share what that was all about?"

"I'm sorry about leaving the restaurant like that."

"Are you okay?"

My shoulders rose slowly and fell quickly. "I will be."

"Let me guess, that was the girl who's had your mind gone these past few months."

I snapped my eyes at her and then softened my look. "I care about her, that's all," I stated, throwing sugar on my words.

"Tell me about her. What's she like?"

"You sure you wanna talk about this? You *just* lost your father. We shouldn't be talking about my shit."

Cena shook her head. "We've both had our share of loss, Kas. And besides, anything is better than talking about death. I've been on autopilot all day. I didn't snap out of it until you chased ol' girl out the door."

"I met her the night Koda died. She was a bottle girl at the club we went to. I knew she was only there for the money. I could tell she wasn't worried about no nigga, not even me, forreal. She was focused. And then she had this fire in her eyes whenever she talked about her design business. I knew I needed someone to wrap up one of my projects, so I met with her a few times and then turned her loose. She's intelligent and funny. I don't know. Watching her flex her creative muscle is a different level of sexy. I ain't never experienced shit like that before."

"And I take it she doesn't know about The Order or us."

"No. I wanted to tell her about us, but it just never felt like the right time. There was so much push and pull between us, and when I finally got her, today happened." I grumbled.

Cena cocked her head to the side. "I thought you said you never wanted to get married."

"I didn't."

"But you would, right? If it were her walking down that aisle to you instead of me?"

I pulled my eyes up to hers without answering. She'd called me out, ripped my heart off my sleeve, and tossed it on front street. Silence hung between us before she craned her neck so that her lips could kiss my cheek.

"I'm sorry you lost your girl, but—"

"I'm sorry you lost your father," I interjected.

"Kasim, let me finish."

"My fault."

"I'm sorry you lost your girl, but if you love her the way I think you do, you'll let her go. It's the only way to protect her from families like ours."

I forced a half smile while wagging my head back and forth. "I knew that it would come to this."

In many ways, she was right. Cena understood the power that came with being a legacy in The Order. Things with her would be easy, maybe even carefree in some ways, but she just wasn't Jrue.

* * *

I RETURNED HOME, and the first thing I noticed when I stepped inside my bedroom was the bed. She'd made it before she left. My eyes transferred to the folded note on my pillow before I walked over to read it.

So much for being professional. ;-)
-Jrue

I sighed before tossing the note on my nightstand and went to take a shower. Warm water cascaded from my rain showerhead before I dunked my head underneath it, allowing it to flow all over my body. No matter how much soap I used, or hard I scrubbed, I couldn't wash off the feeling of defeat. I had Jrue right where I wanted her and still fumbled her heart. I didn't know if she would ever speak to me again, but I had to keep trying.

I yawned before laying my head against my pillow. Seconds later, I rolled over and buried my face in the sheets where she was when I'd left. Everything still smelled like her. Had they not been cold, I would've sworn she was still here... beside me, where she should've fuckin' been in the first place. Our sex was still on replay in my mind, tattooed against my thoughts. Her sweet kisses and the warmth of her body pressed against mine were like drugs to me. I closed my eyes, and views of her continued to dance through my head, first landing on the night before when I had her legs wrapped around my beard, then on our conversation at the carnival we'd spent the day at, weeks prior.

"The love has to feel like nineties RnB. If it doesn't, then I don't want it," she told me.

"What do you mean by that?"

"I don't know; I guess I've always been kind of an old soul at heart. Like, If I'm in a relationship with you and we beefin', I don't want an

apology through text. I don't wanna talk it out over FaceTime. I want a sincere, to my face, slow jam, I'm sorry mixtape type of apology."

"Oh, so you wanna nigga down on bended knee and shit?" I chuckled.

Jrue playfully punched my arm. "Exactly! I enjoy the tradition of being courted and wooed and made to feel special instead of being made to feel like a piece of ass."

Somehow sleep managed to find me as flashbacks of each minute I shared with Jrue flashed through my head.

* * *

I WOKE up missing Jrue even more than I did before I went to sleep. It was some shit I didn't know was possible. It was crazy how much of a hold she had on me. I didn't admit it to her face, but Cena was right. If it were Jrue meeting me at the altar, I would've been happy to give her my last name. Groggy, I staggered into the kitchen to pour myself a drink.

I was already a fool over her, and I knew liquor wouldn't do shit but push me over the edge. But I didn't care. I was addicted to everything about her. Three drinks later, I was past my limit and far from sober. I pulled my phone out to call her. The minute I put it up to my ear, it went straight to voicemail. I knew she'd blocked me hours prior, but I tried anyway. I'd become toxic, obsessed even. It was my first time discovering what it felt like to unravel over someone since my brother was killed. No. Unraveling was too graceful. I was spiraling.

Since I couldn't get her on the phone, I decided to pull up at her crib. My sobriety was questionable, but I didn't care. I would've gone to the moon to see her if I had to. I set my glass down and searched for my keys before realizing I didn't want to show up empty-handed.

Jrue had made it clear that she wasn't the type to be wooed with jewelry and bags. She required a nigga to think past all the materialistic shit and get to the meat of my feelings. I picked up my glass of cognac again and went into the living room to crack open my laptop.

Another hour and a half passed, and I'd taken the time to curate the perfect playlist to grab her attention while telling her how I felt. I added The Tony Rich Project and Case for sincerity, a little Aaliyah for love and devotion, and Jay-Z and Blackstreet for a bit of grit and nostalgia. The entire drive over to her spot, I kept replaying what I would say to her—how profusely I would apologize. There were so many things I needed to get off my chest. The moment my fist collided with her front door, everything I'd tried to remember from the car disappeared from my head.

"Is she here?" I questioned.

"She doesn't want to see you. Go home to your fiancée," her roommate responded.

"Can I please talk to her, Yara? It is Yara, right? Please, I just need a minute to explain."

"Nigga, you can't come in!" She bucked.

"Listen, I know you're just doing your job as her girl and all, but I gotta talk to her. I didn't mean for her to get caught up in all this dramatic shit."

Yara gave me a cold shrug. "I don't know what to tell you."

"Can you please give her this?"

She looked down at the box extending from my hand to hers. "I don't think she will want whatever this is."

"Please, just try."

"Sure," she said before closing the door in my face.

I kept picturing Jrue held up in her bedroom, her heart breaking into a million pieces because of me. Her entire world was crushed, and I couldn't even explain why. I left Jrue's apartment more upset than when I arrived. All I could do was pray she listened to it and found it in her heart to hear me out. In the meantime, I needed to blow off steam and kill something or someone.

Three

CANAAN

I STARED at my hazy reflection in the steamy bathroom mirror before wiping my hand across the glass. The steam exited the bathroom alongside me as I trekked into my closet to throw on something to wear to my father's funeral. I never planned to kill him... at least not at first. Saying the thought hadn't crossed my mind would be a lie, but it was never planned. Julius was the first person I called the night I left my father's house. He told me to go home and burn the clothes I had on, go out to the club as if things were normal, and see him after. As requested, I showed up hours later, only to see Kamil pop up there too. Julius told him I had news about the Simms family to throw him off. Cena had been calling and texting me non-stop, but I'd been avoiding her. It wasn't until later that morning I called her back and pretended to be shocked about the news of our father being stabbed. The most shocking part was that he was still hanging on. I was on the phone with her when he took his last breath. In a way, I felt like I showed him mercy. The cancer ate away at his body slowly, and my actions gave him a quicker ticket out.

. . .

SNAPPING BACK INTO THE PRESENT, I swiped up my phone and reread all the texts I'd sent the night before while lighting a fresh blunt. I knew I couldn't get through the day without a lot of drugs in my system, so I went partying the night before and got zooted on weed, Perc, and liquor. I was leaning and swaying like a hippie underneath the strobe lights—anything to clear the thoughts from my mind and ease the pain. I'd hit Trinity's and Yara's phones in the wee hours of the morning, and neither texted me back.

Me to Trinity: *I'm fucked up.*
Me to Trinity: *I wanna see you and my son, but I'm fucked up right now.*
Me to Trinity: *Trin. Hit me back. I wanna talk.*

I shook my head before clicking Yara's name and reading those messages.

Me to Yara: *I wanna taste it.*
Me to Yara: *Come sit that pretty pussy on my face.*

My head hung low as I texted both of them the exact copy and pasted apology message.

Me: *Yo. Last night was a blur. I was dealing with a lot of shit. I still am. I'm sorry if I said anything out the way.*

* * *

AN HOUR BEFORE THE SERVICE, close family members and some of the leaders in The Order gathered at my father's house, while his soldiers convened at the church. Now that my father was gone, I knew it wouldn't be long before his wishes to make Cena the new head of our family came to fruition. My sister and I hadn't spoken since I left the hospital the day he died, and I wasn't looking forward to sitting next to her ass on the way to the church or sharing a pew at the funeral. The hearse and four limos arrived, and dozens of blood-red roses were loaded inside the hearse.

Cena pulled away a single rose before we filed into the first limo. Once inside, she held the rose up to her nose and drew in a deep breath. "Mom loved roses," she said.

"I remember."

I stared out of the window, zoned out to thoughts of my mother. The news of her breast cancer came a few weeks after Cena and I turned sixteen. Months later, she'd beat it and was in remission. Everything was good for the next two years, almost as if nothing had ever happened, like it was a blip in the system. Then, a year later, it returned with a vengeance and took her out within eight months. It had been six years since she died, and I hadn't touched a rose since.

"You plan on speaking to me anytime soon?" Cena asked, jarring me back to the present.

"The fuck you want me to say?" I quizzed before pulling my blunt and lighter out of my suit jacket pocket and cracking the window.

She sighed while rolling her eyes to the sunroof. "You know you can't smoke in here."

"Watch me," I defied her.

"Listen, I know Pop told you about his intentions to have me take over for the head of our families in The Order."

"And?"

"Nothing."

I turned my attention toward the window and hit the button to roll it up. Sometime during our ride, it started to rain. Drizzles slid down the window, obscuring the view as I puffed. Soon, the entire back end of the limo was filled with thick, wavy smoke. "Nah, go ahead and say what you gotta say."

"Today's not the day for me to ask you what I want to ask you, Canaan."

My brow raised in suspicion. "And what's that?"

"Did you have anything to do with it?"

"Why in the fuck would you ask me some shit like that? He was my fuckin' father, too, you know? Ask Lorraine! She said goodnight to me when I left. And when I left, he was alive. What you need to be doing is questioning her a little harder instead of pointing your fuckin' finger at me!"

"I didn't mean to upset you. I'm just trying to get to the bottom of all this."

"Bullshit! You knew damn well that was gon' piss me off, and you did it anyway to get a reaction out of me! If you want someone to blame for this, make sure you look somewhere the hell else," I warned her.

Once again, the car fell silent for a few minutes before Cena's voice called out to me again. "Now that he's gone, we need to talk about next steps..."

I scoffed. "The man ain't even in his grave yet, and you wanna talk about next steps. You don't know the first thing about what it takes to be the fuckin' head of this family!"

"You don't know what I know."

"I know you ain't never gotten your fuckin' hands dirty. That was my job, right? Imagine how I feel for thinkin' me and this nigga were bonding for the past twenty-five years, and the entire time he was treatin' me no better than the fuckin' help. He wasn't molding me into anything but a fuckin' expendable soldier," I griped, expelling smoke out my nostrils as I spoke.

"I'm sure he had his reasons."

My brow furrowed. "You think he gave enough of a fuck to explain his reasons to me? Huh? When you gon' wake up and realize that nigga never gave a fuck about me? His own blood! Guess I don't blame you, though. Took me twenty-five years to figure the shit out."

"Canaan, I'm sorry, okay?"

"Not sorry enough to step aside, though, right, sis?"

She had me wishing I had my gun on me to solve my problems once and for all. I'd already taken out my father. One bullet for my sister, and everything would be over. I would be on top and have everything I wanted. But I knew that was too easy.

The limo ride grew quiet. I watched her remove the red rose from her lap and place it on the seat beside her. "Look, Canaan, I—"

"Did he tell you about his gambling debts?" I interjected, uninterested in hearing what she was about to say.

"Yes."

"Did you know if your wedding doesn't pan out, then he's planning to marry me off to Ruiz Rivera's fuckin' daughter?"

Cena's almond-shaped eyes widened. She was surprised but wouldn't dare admit that our *dear ol' dad* had even kept her in the dark about some things. Before she could respond, the limo stopped in front of the church. Instead of waiting for her answer, I exited the limo. Clouds covered the gray sky as a cold, dewy sensation cloaked my skin. The slick, wet pavement, combined with the dampness of the air, made the entire scene somber. I passed by people standing outside the church. No one cracked a smile, not even a forced one; it reminded me of the day we buried my mother. The open gold casket was the first thing my eyes landed on inside the sanctuary. I pinged my eyes to anything in the room but him lying there. I didn't know if I was ready to see my father one last time or if I even wanted to, considering. Instead, I focused on the two big, red rose arrangements sitting on each side of his casket, the funeral program with his best picture printed on it, and the plush red church carpet underneath my leather Prada loafers. Soon enough, the pews filled with family, different ranking organization members, and more people who'd come to pay their respects.

"I hate everything about this. Why did he have to die? I–I still can't believe it," Cena whispered to me after the funeral director closed the casket and the service officially started.

I chose not to respond. My anger for him may not have been well-known to everyone in the room, but it was real. She reached out to grab my hand, and I froze, unable to pull away from her grasp. Cena and I held hands while she sobbed silently through the entire service. From time to time, Kasim would reach up to place his hand on her shoulder to console her. Instead of sitting beside us, he, Julius, Kamil, and his wife sat in the row behind us. When the final prayer concluded, I let go to join the other five pallbearers chosen to carry out his body alongside me. Little did they know, I was carrying more than my father's heavy gold box on my shoulders. Family and friends followed us out with flowers, preparing to reconvene at the gravesite. As soon as we slid my father's casket into the hearse, shots rang through the air like church bells.

Instincts on a thousand, I hit the slick, black pavement. People scattered like leaves in the wind; screams amplified as they took cover. My father's soldiers stayed strapped, retaliating outside of the church immediately. I glanced back at Cena, who was hovering on the ground. Kas was shielding her from the bullets. Rain puddles jumped and rippled as shots continued to echo through the open, damp air. My eyes then moved in the direction the screams were coming from. Janessa Underwood was screaming, trying to get to her father's side while Kamil tried his best to keep her safe. Without our weapons, we were all powerless. I looked over at Xavier Underwood, Janessa's father, bleeding on the ground. A mixture of random wet raindrops and blood discolored the concrete beneath him.

"Oh my God! Somebody call nine-one-one! Please call nine-one-one!" Janessa bawled.

* * *

MY BLOOD WAS STILL BOILING when I got home later that night. Someone knew the major players of The Order would all be in one place and had tried to take us all out, which meant *no one* was safe. After the chaos outside of my father's funeral, Cena was so shaken up that we decided it was best to cancel the burial and repass and have a private burial for the immediate family later. I turned the key into the lock and opened the door to see Trinity standing in the middle of my living room floor with her arms tucked underneath her full, C-cup breasts. I paused my already sluggish stride. "Trin? What the f–what the hell are you doing here?"

She pushed her thick, burgundy-red dreads away from her face. "Oh, you needed and wanted to see me at three o'clock this morning. But now that I show up unannounced, it's what am I doing here?"

I shook my head. "It's not like that. Today was just a long fuckin' day, aight."

Her honey-brown face scrunched up as she gave me a onceover. "Yeah? Well, me too. What happened to you anyway? Why do your clothes look like that?"

My chin dropped while glancing down at the wrinkles in my clothes and creases in my designer loafers. A scoff escaped my lips. "There was a shootout at my father's funeral today. I almost didn't make it home to have this fuckin' conversation with your ass! You know I gave you my spare key for emergencies only. What the fuck is going on? Huh? Where's my son?" I yelled.

"W–what. Your father's funeral? You never told me anything about him dying, Canaan. When did this happen? I would've been here for you if I knew you were going through some heavy shit like this."

"I'm fine. Where is Za, Trinity? Where's my son?"

"Lower your voice, aight? *Our* son is fine. He's in your bed asleep."

A sigh of relief pushed through my nostrils. "Aight. I'm going to go take a shower."

"Wait a minute, Canaan. We need to talk about this! You just told me that you buried your father and almost lost your life in the same breath, and now you just want to walk off and shower like everything is cool. What's going on with you? I'm trying to be here for you if you'll let me."

"I don't wanna talk about this shit. Not now and not with you."

I walked past her without saying another word and looked in on Za before going into the bathroom and closing the door. He was my carbon copy and the best part of me. I was mad that I was so fucked up in the head that I wasn't able to greet his mother the way I wanted to, the way I should've. But she'd taken me by surprise, and I'd already had enough surprises for one day. Water poured from the showerhead as I undressed while silently unpacking my day. In my family's line of work, showing weakness was like pouring a trail of kerosene and waiting for someone to come along and light the match. It wasn't a question of *if* we would retaliate but when.

After my shower, I went from the bedroom to the living room to see Trinity curled up on the couch, pretending to watch TV. I went into the kitchen to pour myself a drink, eyeing her from across the room without speaking. She'd gone and swept her long dreads up into a large bun on the top of her head, bringing even more attention to her beautiful face. Even from feet away, I could tell she'd gotten her lashes done. Tattoos covered her right shoulder down to her hand. One of them was my name.

Before I could leave the kitchen, she walked over to me. I looked into her sultry brown eyes before complimenting her. "You look good as shit," I said before kissing her tattooed right hand.

"I know."

"You ready to tell me why you packed up Za and left Rhode Island to come all the way here?"

"Do you still think I assume you're not happy I did?"

I pushed out a long, slow sigh while she wrapped her arms around my neck and pulled me into a consoling hug. I set my glass down on the counter before fully embracing her. Her energy was warm, calm, and everything I didn't know I needed. My hands found their way down her tiny waist before my palms skimmed over his thick hips and ass. Touching her curves was like second nature to me. She had the type of presence I could see myself growing soft in if she stayed around too long, and I couldn't afford that.

She moved my hands before prying herself away from me. "You don't quit, huh?"

"I'm sorry. I'll behave."

"Anyway, I came here today because Za was in an accident at school."

My brows raised to my hairline. "He what?"

"Calm down, Canaan. He's okay," she assured me." You know he's a tough kid."

"What the hell happened?"

"He was playing outside at recess when he and another boy ran into each other headfirst and fell. His teacher said both boys got the wind knocked out of them, and the nurse gave them ice packs for their heads. He's got a pretty big knot on his forehead, so I took him to urgent care to make sure he didn't have a concussion. He kept crying about how much he wanted to see you. I didn't think a few minutes over FaceTime would remedy it this time around, so I took the spare key you gave me and came down."

I sighed. "Damn, man. You aight?"

"As long as he's fine, I'm fine. But enough about me. Why didn't you tell me your father died, Canaan?"

My shoulders rose and fell. "I don't know. It's not like this shit is easy to talk about."

"Things never are with you."

"Look, if you tryna start some shit tonight, I'm lettin' you know right now, I'm not in the mood."

"I'm not trying to start anything. If you weren't so busy being defensive, maybe you would see I'm trying to be here for you."

My eyes dropped to the floor. "You right. I'm sorry."

"I get it if you don't want to talk about it, but I am here for you, Canaan."

"Thanks," I replied before pulling her into another tight hug.

"It just sucks that Za never got to meet his grandfather."

That thought hadn't crossed my mind before then. Knowing who my father was, especially in his last days, Za was better off not knowing shit about him. "Yeah," I responded. "How long are you two stayin'?"

"I figured we'd stay for a couple of days before making the trip back."

"Oh. Okay."

"Wow."

My brows creased. "What?"

"That was your chance to say that we *didn't* need to go back and that we could finally stay here with you in the same fuckin' city and that things would be—you know what, never mind. You're already not in the mood, and I'm not trying to make shit worse. I'm gonna go lay down in the back with Za," she said, smacking her glossed, pouty lips.

"Hold up a minute, Trin."

"No, Canaan. It's clear now ain't the time to put my feelings on you when you dealin' with your own shit. I don't like it, but I can respect it."

"What you want from me, T, huh?"

"I've made it painfully clear what I want from you, and you've made it clear I'll never get it."

My lungs thrust out a frustrated sigh. She was pushing me into a corner, and I didn't like that shit. I cared about Trinity more than I'd ever cared about anyone. She had my seed. As my son's mother, no one could take her place in my heart.

"Listen to me when I say that stressing you out isn't my intention."

"Yeah, well, you sure got a funny way of showing it. All you do is leave me in the dark about shit."

"It's better that way. Trust me."

She began to massage her neck, scrunching up the red ink etched into the side. "You always say that, and to be honest with you, as badly as you don't wanna hear this shit, I'm tired, Canaan. I'm tired of being stuck out in Rhode Island away from my family, away from you."

"And I've been tellin' you time and time again that I'm waiting for the right time. Things can't always be how you want them, when you want them."

"I'm not sayin' it has to be, but none of this has been going my way for the past five years. Did you hear what I just said, Canaan? I've been holding you down, being patient for five fuckin' years, and I'm done. You can keep your key when Za and I leave," she announced.

"Oh, now you don't want my key no more?"

"I won't be needing it."

"And why the fuck not?"

"Because we're moving back to New York to be near my family. I gave you five years to figure this shit out or make whatever moves you had to make or plans you had come into play. I'm done."

Her last two words sank what was left of my icy heart. A pregnant pause divided our conversation before she spun around on her bare feet to walk away. I reached out to stop her by catching her swinging arm.

"Trinity."

She snatched her arm away. "No. I don't wanna talk anymore. I said what I had to say."

"And so that's it then? You say what you gotta say, and that's the end of the fuckin' conversation?"

"Unless you plan on sayin' or doin' somethin' to change my mind, then yeah. That's it," she assured me quickly before stepping away.

"I already lost my fuckin' father, T. I can't lose you too," I confessed to her back.

"Then give me a reason to stay, Canaan. A real one."

I sighed. Over the years, Trinity had gained a high-level understanding of The Order and my family's drug organization. But she'd never met one of my family members, and she didn't know all the ins and outs of my daily business dealings.

"I want you here. I want you both here. If New York is where you wanna be, then I'll move out there if I have to. Please, just don't leave," I pleaded. Truth be told, I just wanted to feel better.

"As nice as it sounds, that's not enough for me anymore. You're like a broken record, sayin' the same shit over and over again, and I'm done being the dummy that keeps listening."

"I killed my father for us, Trinity. So we could be together," I confided. The words spilled out of my mouth before I could stop them.

Her eyes widened. "That's not funny, Canaan."

"I'm not joking."

"Y–you what?"

"You heard me."

"Yeah, I heard you, but did you really do it for the reason you say you did? For us?"

I nodded my head. "Yeah. What? Are you scared of me now? Now that you know, you wanna run away?" I accused.

She inched closer to me. "No."

"You sure about that? Because it sounded like you had one foot out the door a minute ago."

"Shut up. I'm sure."

"Good, because now that he's gone," I paused, "there's nothin' stopping me from being with you and giving you the family you want... the one you deserve."

Her perfectly sculpted brows creased in confusion. "What are you saying?"

"Marry me."

Her breath jerked in her throat. "W–what?"

"Marry me, Trinity."

"Again, this isn't funny," she articulated.

"And again, I'm bein' dead ass serious. Will you fuckin' marry a nigga?"

Tears welled up in the corners of her eyes before she nodded. "Y–yes."

"I'll call the jeweler in the morning and have him come over. You can pick out whatever ring you want."

She crashed into my arms before tossing her lean, tattooed arms around my neck. "Oh my God. I'm sorry for doubting you. I love you, Canaan. I love you so much!"

Four

JRUE

RIHANNA'S "LOVE ON THE BRAIN" echoed through my speaker as the warm water rolled down my curves. The week had flown by. It was as if I blinked and it was almost Friday, which meant Kas's wedding day was coming up. Whatever time I spent not working on building my clientele was spent eating my feelings and sleeping. I toyed with the idea of plugging in the flash drive he'd delivered almost daily, but I couldn't bring myself to do it. Whatever was on it wouldn't change the fact that he lied. Before my thoughts spiraled out of control, there was a knock on the bathroom door.

"Hey. It's me," Yara announced from the other side.

"Yeah?"

She opened the door just as I shut off the shower. "Just letting you know I ordered pizza. A bitch is starving."

I nodded before wrapping my towel around me and pushing the curtain back. "Cool."

"I got your favorite. Half pepperoni, half pineapple."

The corner of my mouth rose slightly. "Thanks."

"Ugh," she groaned. "What's it gonna take for you to get out of your funky breakup feelings?"

My shoulders rose and fell. "I don't know what you mean. I'm good," I protested.

"We both know you lying, but I'm all here for the denial too, sis."

"Damn, speaking of sis, I need to call Charity back. Thanks for the reminder."

"No problem. I'll find you when the pizza gets here."

"Okay. Thanks again."

"No problem."

The door closed behind her before I said, "Hey, Siri, call Char."

"*Calling Char mobile,*" my phone responded.

The phone rang a few times before my little brat of a sister answered. "Hey, ugly."

"Your mama."

She smacked her lips. "She yo' mama, too, *fool.*"

"Yeah, yeah. Where she at? Work?"

"You know she can never seem to say no to picking up extra shifts at the hospital. It's been like that since..."

I nodded. "Yeah. I know."

Our mother had been a registered pediatric nurse for over twenty-five years. Growing up, our mother always made sure she was home for every bedtime bath and a goodnight kiss—she and our father both. When he passed away three years ago from a heart attack, she started throwing herself into her work more, saying it was because she couldn't be at home where he wasn't and that there was always a baby and a family that she could be helping instead of grieving at home. So, on the nights she chose to work late, I made sure Charity was safe, had eaten, had done her homework, and could get back and forth to her volleyball practices and games.

"Anyway," I said, snapping back to the present, "did you get the email with the DNA test results?"

"Yeah."

"You ready to look at them?"

"Yeah. Hold on. Let me FaceTime you real quick."

I swiped to answer her call and then pulled up the email on my phone. "Okay. What does yours say?" I mumbled while scanning over mine.

"I don't think I know what any of this means. It's just a lot of percentages."

"Okay, wait. Look at your ancestry composition. What do you have for Sub-Saharan African? Like, what's your percentage?"

"Oh, um, eighty percent."

"And your European?"

"Uh, twelve percent."

"Hmm."

"What? What's yours say?" she asked.

"What about your East Asian and Native American?" I continued.

"Less than one percent."

"What the hell?"

"What? What's wrong with yours? What does yours say, Jrue?" she quizzed.

I huffed, still baffled as to why none of our percentages were that close. "Um, can you tell me what your highest African percentage was?"

"Nigerian at over twenty-six percent. Why do you keep asking me all these questions but aren't answering any of mine? I'm not telling you anything else."

"Shut up. I'm just trying to figure this out."

"Figure what out, Jrue? You're not telling me anything!"

"I'm seventy-five percent Sub-Saharan African. My highest percentage is Southern East African. My European is over twenty percent, and my East Asian and Native American are over one percent. It doesn't make any sense."

"We're sisters. Why doesn't it match?"

"I don't know, Charity. That's what I've been saying." I huffed.

"Maybe you didn't spit in the little tube correctly. Or maybe they mixed up your DNA in the lab with somebody else's!" she theorized.

"Shut up."

"I'm just saying. Oh, wait!"

"What?"

"I told mom that one of my friends got the test for me, and she told me that she and Dad did theirs a few years before he died."

"Yeah? Does she still have the results?"

"I don't know. Why?"

"Because this doesn't make any sense. Maybe seeing theirs will shed some light on why mine doesn't match up with yours a little closer. Maybe I got more of Mom's genes than Dad's or something."

"Yeah, maybe."

"Can you go look?"

"I wouldn't know where to begin, Jrue."

"Go upstairs to Mom's closet and look in the back. She keeps all our important papers in one of Dad's old shoe boxes. That's where I went when I looked for my birth certificate that day."

"Well, did you see any DNA results in there?"

"I don't know because that's not what I was looking for at the time. I'm telling you where to look; if they aren't there, I'll drop it."

"Ugh, fine."

Charity rummaged around the box inside Mom's closet for a few minutes. "Oh, wait. I think I found something."

"What is it?"

"It's their DNA test results."

"Read it to me!" I exclaimed.

"Okay, okay. Chill out."

"Take a picture of them and send them to me!"

"I'm not doing all that. Just give me a second."

"It takes two seconds to snap a picture, Char. Just do it."

She smacked her lips. "You're so annoying. Hold on."

I got two pictures a few minutes later and quickly compared them to mine. "See a match with either of them?"

I reluctantly shook my head. "No, nothing."

"Damn, Jrue! I always knew you were adopted!" she teased.

"Shut up! That's not funny. You look like both Mom and Dad, and I don't look like either of them."

"You're being dramatic. You look like Mom sometimes, kinda."

"Ugh. I'll call you back," I told her before ending the call.

After getting dressed, I grabbed my laptop and went down the rabbit hole of DNA ancestry and what it meant since it seemed I didn't match with the rest of my family members. Within my first few Google searches, I learned that full siblings only shared about half of the same

DNA, but that still didn't explain why I didn't match either of my parents.

Me: *I think we should get a blood test done.*
Char: *Are you for real right now?*
Me: *Yeah. You down?*
Char: *Sure. Yeah. I guess. Whatever.*
Me: *Good. And don't tell Mom.*

I put the phone down just as Yara knocked on my bedroom door. "Hey. The pizza is here, but I gotta pee. Can you get the door? I already paid through the app."

"Yeah, sure."

I closed my laptop before darting to the front door. I swung it open to see a delivery man holding a large vase with over three dozen long-stem roses instead of a couple of large pizzas. "Um, I think you've got the wrong address," I told him.

"Are you, uh, Jrue Norwood?" he asked.

"Yes."

"Then these are for you. Where would you like me to put them?"

"Uh," I paused, "on the counter over there is fine."

"Thanks. You have a good evening."

"Yeah, um. You too."

"I see that wasn't the pizza," Yara said, making her way over to the roses.

"Nope."

"There's a card. You wanna read it?"

"No. I already know who they are from."

"Fine. If you won't read the card, I will."

"Well?" I inquired.

"Well, what?"

"Tell me what it said."

"Thought you weren't interested in seeing the card," she teased while waving it in front of my face.

"Stop playing, Ya-Ya. I'm not in the mood for games right now."

"Oh, hush. It just says *I'm sorry*."

I scoffed. "Wow. Classic."

"I mean, how you gon' act, Jrue?"

My forehead wrinkled. "What do you mean? You think I'm supposed to hop back on his line because he sent me a few plants?"

"You petty, and you know it." She snickered.

I sighed. "I don't know. My mind is a little all over the place right now. I think something is seriously wrong with me."

"What do you mean?"

"Charity begged me to get these DNA test kits, so I did. Then when we started going over our results over the phone a little while ago, nothing matched up."

"Okay. Is that a bad thing?"

"No, not exactly, but it doesn't explain why I don't match up with either of my parent's results."

Yara folded her arms across her chest. "What are you saying, Jrue?"

"I'm saying... Well, I don't know what I'm saying. What I hope I'm not saying is that I'm adopted..."

Yara's eyes widened. "No. I don't think that. You look like your... well, everybody doesn't look like their parents, Jrue. That doesn't mean you're not their daughter. Try not to overthink it."

"I'm trying not to, but this is scary. Like, what if I'm not who I think I've been this entire time? To go from thinking you know who all your aunts and uncles are to realizing it all might not be true, that's a shitty pill to have to swallow."

"You're right, but how about you don't overreact until you have to?"

I nodded. "Okay, okay. Well, what about you?"

"What do you mean?"

"You know what I mean. What's up with you? I know I've been lickin' my own wounds lately, but no more ducking and dodging me, girl! You need to fill me in on your life and tell me what's been going on with you!"

She sighed, shoulders sagging. "I don't even know where to begin."

"Start anywhere."

"I fucked up, Jrue. I fucked up *bad*," she said, swiping tears from her cheeks.

"W–what happened? What's wrong?"

"I'm pregnant," she blurted out before covering her eyes with her hands.

My brows shot up. "You're what!"

Her hands slowly slid down her face. "Before you start jumping for joy and shit, Nate doesn't know. No one does except you."

I smiled. "Okay, well, I'm honored."

"Don't be. You haven't heard the whole story."

"If you're about to tell me what positions you did to conceive, I'm going to throw up," I warned her.

She rolled her eyes skyward. "That's not what I was going to say at all."

"Then what is it?"

"Nate doesn't know because I'm ninety-nine percent sure the baby isn't his."

My stomach twisted in knots. "W–what do you mean the baby isn't his? If it's not his, then whose is it? And why don't I already know about him?"

Her eyes shined with tears as she sighed. "I know. I'm sorry. I was keeping shit tight. Shit was cool 'til it wasn't, y'know? Now it's all so fuckin' messy."

"How messy we talkin'?"

Instead of responding, she pulled out her phone to pull up a picture of him and showed it to me. "This is him."

I frowned, immediately recognizing him as the nigga from the club I went off on the night I quit. "Are you serious?"

Her brows raised. "Yeah, why?"

"You remember the night I quit Bliss, and I told you about the nigga I went off on because he got handsy with me in VIP?"

"Are you kidding me? That was him?"

"Yeah."

"Are you sure that was Canaan?"

"Oh my God, yes! That was his name! Are you fuckin' kidding me, Ya-Ya? How did you even run into a nigga like him?"

She sighed. "Oh my God, this is embarrassing. Okay, so you remember some months ago when I got into that little fender bender?"

"You mean when you hit that car at the gas station?"

"Yeah. So, I told you half the story."

"What exactly did you leave out?" I asked.

"Okay, so you know I hit his car. You know we both got out to check our cars, and then..."

"You told me he said you were good, and you left."

"He *did* say I was good, and I *did* leave, but not before he asked me for my number. I told him I had a man, and then he was like, damn, maybe I should call my insurance company after all. And I'm like, hold up, are you serious? Then he told me he was joking. We laughed and legit talked for like another fifteen minutes. I did give him my number, and then one thing led to another... and yeah. We've been sort of, uh, no strings attached fuck buddies for the past few months."

My brows heightened. "No shit, Sherlock. Now look at you!"

"Ugh, I know! I know! I feel terrible!"

"How far along are you?"

"I–I don't know for sure. I found out a week and a half ago when I realized I was late. But that's not even the fucked-up part."

"What else is there, girl? Damn!" I exclaimed, unsure if I could handle any more.

"I found out that he lied to me about his last name. He told me his last name was Mitchell when it was McQueen."

"McQueen? Why do I feel like I've heard that name?"

Yara shot me a regretful look. "Because you have. He's Cena McQueen's brother, Kasim's fiancée."

My fingers splayed out against my breastbone, and my eyes widened in complete shock. "Are you fuckin' with me? Tell me you're fuckin' with me."

"I wish I were, but I'm not."

I sighed. "This is..."

"A lot, I know." She finished my sentence before the doorbell rang. "I'll get it this time."

Yara walked to the door and returned with a couple of pizzas a few minutes later. "I hope the baby doesn't make me regret this pizza, but I've been craving this greasy goodness all damn day."

"So, yeah. Back to the baby. How do you feel about it? Like, do you wanna keep it? Are you planning on telling Nate?"

Her voice shook. "I–I don't know what I want. I wish I did, but I don't."

"I mean, are you going to go to the doctor and find out how far along you are? And you're one hundred percent sure there's no way Nate could be the father?"

She shook her head. "I'm sure."

"Then what about Canaan? Are you going to tell him?"

Her head wagged from side to side again. "No. For what? He's clearly a liar."

"A liar with funds, obviously. Didn't you say Cena was spending crazy money on the wedding?"

"Yeah, but I don't know. I–I don't know. I'll figure something out."

"Well, whatever you choose to do, I'm here to support you," I said before pulling her into a comforting hug.

* * *

A COUPLE of beers and a few slices of pizza later, I was in my room knee-deep in article after article on ancestry and ethnicity results. By the time I closed my laptop, my head was swimming with so much information I didn't know what to do with it. There was no way I would go and talk Yara's ear off some more about it after finding out about her situation. Then suddenly, my thoughts landed on Kas and then the flash drive.

"Fuck it," I muttered before pulling the box out of my nightstand drawer.

I cracked open my laptop and pushed the flash drive into the USB port. When I clicked on the file, a playlist with almost half a dozen songs appeared. First was "Nobody Knows" by The Tony Rich Project, followed by "Song Cry" by Jay-Z, "Don't Leave Me" by Blackstreet, "One in a Million" by Aaliyah, and "Missing You" by Case. With tears rolling down my cheeks, I picked up my phone to unblock his number before going to my messages. I hoped the text would be worth my while and not the instant regret I had a feeling it would be.

Me: *90's RnB with a splash of hip-hop, huh? Classic. Oh, and thanks for the roses.*

The three ellipses populated on the screen before disappearing. Seconds later, he was calling. My posture immediately stiffened before my thumb slid against the screen to accept. "Y–yeah?" I answered, voice unsteady and uncertain.

"You're welcome, Jrue."

"What made you do all of that?"

"You left me no other way to contact you, so I had to take it old school."

I scoffed. "Flowers shouldn't be considered old school, but the gesture still stands."

"Weren't you the one who said that if the love didn't feel like nineties RnB, you ain't want it? And you wanted mixtapes over Birkins and shit when you break up with a nigga."

"I wasn't aware we were ever together to break up."

He sighed into the receiver. "It's good to hear your voice, Jrue."

"Yeah, well, thanks again. Goodnight."

"You goin' to sleep?"

"No. Why?"

"You think we could talk?"

"About?"

"C'mon, Jrue. You and I both know there's some shit we gotta get off our chests to each other. Say whatever you gotta say to me. I can take it. I promise you that."

"Listen, I have too much on my mind right now to even try to deal with my feelings for you."

"What's on your mind?"

"Nothing. It's nothing. Why do you care anyway? Shouldn't you be more concerned with your fiancée?" I snapped.

"Because I care about you, Jrue. And whenever you're ready to talk about us and my situation, let me know."

"What if I'm never ready?"

"I'm a patient man. Now tell me what's on your mind."

I sighed, unable to fight the urge to spill everything on my mind.

"So, my younger sister talked me into doing this DNA ancestry shit. We got the results today, and we aren't anything alike. And then I found the ancestry results from the test my parents took some years ago, and I don't match up with either of them. So I've been reading like a million articles trying to make sense of it all."

"What all did you learn so far?"

"Well, for starters, you get fifty percent of your mom's genes and fifty percent of your dad's genes, so it's not so uncommon that my DNA doesn't exactly mirror theirs or my sister's, because each egg and sperm basically has a random grab bag of genes. So there could be half of either of their genes that I just didn't get."

"So it sounds like you got your answer then."

"Not exactly."

"What do you mean?"

I pushed out an extended exhale. "I can't explain it. It's just this unsettling feeling in my stomach. Haven't been able to shake it since earlier."

"What are you unsettled about? You think your parents might not be your parents? Like you're adopted or somethin'?"

"I don't know, maybe. It would explain why I don't really favor anyone in my family. I never harped on the thought of it before, but now.... I don't know. Everything seems like a possibility. My life is already turned upside down. What's one more loop-de-loop?" I griped.

"Well, then, what's next? You gon' sleep on it? Keep reading until you dizzy or what?"

"Yeah, I'm over all the extra reading for the night. I told my sister we should get a blood test, but I don't know; maybe I was being dramatic. Shit, maybe you're right. Maybe I'll sleep on it."

"This shit really got your head gone, huh?"

"Yeah. It does."

"Regardless of the outcome or whatever you decide to do, don't let some random ass test dictate your life. You know who raised you. You know who your family is. Don't lose sight of all that, getting hung up on a piece of what makes you who you are."

"Wow, there you go."

"What?"

"Nothing. It's nothing. Thanks."

"Nah, tell me."

"You sound like you're in the car. Are you driving?" I quizzed, trying to switch the course of the conversation.

"Don't try to distract me. Tell me what you were about to say."

"Ugh, fine," I groaned. "It's just this charm you have that allows you to say all the right things at the right time. I tried to make myself forget about it, but no such luck."

"You givin' a nigga too much credit."

"I know." The line fell silent for a few uncomfortable seconds before we opened our mouths and let our feelings spill out simultaneously. "Why didn't you tell me you had a fiancée?" I asked.

"Can you please let me explain the whole story?" he queried.

I sighed. "Kas, I—"

"Please? Just let me see you so we can talk. I'll tell you everything."

"Why can't you tell me whatever it is you have to tell me over the phone?" I questioned, hesitant to be alone with him.

"Because what I have to tell you is better said face-to-face."

"Fine. How long until you get here?"

"I can pull up on you in ten," he answered with certainty.

My brows snapped together. "Ten? Like ten minutes?"

"Yeah."

"So you are in the car?"

"Yeah. I'll see you in a minute," he stated before ending the call.

I slowly pulled the phone away from my ear before racing to the bathroom to take the quickest shower of my life. As sad as I was, I wasn't going to allow him to see how physically off my game I'd been.

* * *

KAS ARRIVED at my apartment wearing a black tee and sweatpants, Jordans on his feet, and a couple of gold chains around his neck.

"Hey," he greeted me.

The scent of wood and spices against his blemish-free skin made him smell masculine and alluring. My heart was thumping so hard I thought it would lunge through my chest. "Hey..."

He followed me to my bedroom in silence, and suddenly, there were three of us: him, me, and the elephant. We stood in silence. I could feel his eyes on me while I struggled to maintain eye contact with him. I absently licked my bow-shaped lips while my eyes shifted all around my room without really seeing anything at all.

"So..." I started.

He pushed out a hard sigh. "Jrue, listen, I know the last time we saw each other, that shit looked crazy."

"Are you engaged or not?" I blurted out.

He spoke with hesitation in his speech. "Yes. I'm engaged. But it's not in the way you think."

"What other way is there for me to think? My best friend has been planning *your* wedding for months! Months! You had a million and one opportunities to tell me, and you didn't."

"You don't understand. I wanted to tell you so many times, but... I just didn't know how to say the shit."

"How hard is it to say that you're just like every other nigga who wants his cake and another one too."

"I'm far from every other nigga. And if you allowed me to explain, you'd see that."

Instead of listening, I cut him off. "Wait. Is that why you didn't want me to meet your father? Because you didn't want him to know you were running around on his future daughter-in-law!" I accused.

"The only future daughter-in-law I want him to have is you, Jrue! But I can't because—"

My heart somersaulted in my chest. "Because what! All I'm hearing is one excuse after the other."

"No! All you hear is yourself talking because you wanna be right so fuckin' bad. And the truth is, you don't know shit!" he barked.

I bit my lip in an attempt not to respond so quickly. "Okay. Say what you have to say."

"Yes, I'm engaged, but there's nothing between Cena and me. Our marriage is all business."

"All business? What does that mean? Like arranged or something?"

"By our fathers, yes. At first, she wasn't *my* fiancée, but you remember the night we first met at the club, and there was a shootout?"

I nodded slowly. "Yeah."

"Remember I told you my brother was killed that night?"

"Yeah. You were there for his bachelor party, right?"

"Yeah. Well, she was supposed to marry him, but my father moved me into his place when he died."

My body went completely still before my mouth fell open. "Are you serious right now?"

"I am."

"You expect me to believe that you, a grown-ass man, willingly allowed your father, another grown-ass man, to move you around like some pawn on a chessboard? I'm sorry. No disrespect, but what the hell?"

"I know it sounds crazy, but it's the truth. I'm sorry I didn't tell you sooner, but I've been trying to find a way to get out of this shit ever since I found out," he confessed.

"And did you?"

He shook his head. "No."

"So you're getting married this weekend?"

He nodded slowly before inching closer, erasing the distance between us with each step. I took a half step back... and then another until my back was pressed against my closet door.

"Kas," I breathed out, biting my lip.

"She doesn't love me, and I don't love her," he confirmed.

I extended my arm to stop him. "If neither of you loves the other, then why can't she marry someone else?"

"I asked the same thing, but that's not how shit goes in our families."

"What's so special about her family, and yours for that matter?"

He sighed. "Our families aren't like your average family. We make alliances with other wealthy families."

"Hold up. Alliances? Arranged marriages? What the hell are you and your family into, Kas?" I quizzed.

Instead of answering where he stood, he walked over to my bed and sat at the foot. "My family sells weapons to companies, dealers, international organizations, and the like."

"Weapons like guns?"

"Amongst other things."

"So that's where your money comes from?"

"That, stocks, and my real estate investments," he answered.

"Do you hurt people?"

"If I have to," he replied at the ready.

"Oh."

He extended his arms to grip my waist and pull me toward him. "Are you scared of me?"

"No."

"You sure?"

I nodded, unable to focus on anything other than the warmth of his hands against my exposed stomach. "Yes."

"Your body language says otherwise," he noticed.

I looked down, not realizing I had been holding my elbows tight at my sides. I narrowed my eyes at him, immediately noticing his rum-colored orbs were already centered on me. "I'm not scared of you, Kas," I assured him.

"Good, because I want you."

His hands slowly drove over my curves before he pulled me in closer and placed a kiss on my belly button. "I–in what way?" I breathed.

"In all ways," he answered.

I couldn't believe I knew what I knew and was still considering giving him the pussy. He didn't deserve it, but dammit if I didn't want him. My pussy had been screaming his name since he walked through the door. He looked up at me, silencing my private thoughts.

"Why do you do that?"

"Do what?" I asked, brows knitted.

"Scrunch up your nose like that when you're thinking about shit."

"Why are you staring at me so hard to even notice something like that?" I questioned, flipping him into the hot seat.

"You're too beautiful not to."

I huffed. "Stop."

"Stop what?"

"That! Being you. You're bad for me, and you know it."

"That may be true, but I can't stop being me, especially not when I'm around you."

"What does this even mean for us?"

He shook his head before his shoulders rose and fell. "All I know is that I want you, Jrue. I'll go as far as to say I need you."

"Kas—"

"Please, Jrue."

He rested his head against my stomach, and at first, my hands abstained from touching him, as tempting as it was. And then, without my permission, my fingers roamed over his shoulders before I wrapped my arms around him. We were both lowering our guards for one another, for the first time, with our clothes on, although we both knew the clothes wouldn't last too much longer. My face flushed with lust as Kas began to place soft kisses against my bare stomach while raising my crop top up my spine. I stood there, knees locked in place, anxiously anticipating his next touch or kiss. There was no hiding it. I was still very much dick-drunk and dizzy over him.

He stood to his feet, allowing his over-six-foot stature to hover over me. His lips didn't utter a single word, but I knew everything he was trying to say because I was trying to say the same thing. We were both prisoners of our hearts who had fallen in love with someone we couldn't be with. Kas's soft lips settled over mine, overtaking me with one kiss after another while our limbs entangled against my bed. Our bodies remained anchored to each other while his hands outlined my curves.

He lifted my shirt over my head before pinning me underneath him. I could feel the hardness of his dick pressing against my thigh as he unhooked my bra and wrapped his hands around my breasts. His tongue devoted its' time to each nipple before moving down my stomach. Kas sat up to pull off the rest of my clothes before placing butterfly-soft kisses against my bikini line.

"Mmm." I purred as he pressed his thumb against my clit. My pussy was pulsating.

Kas pushed my knees up to my chest and dove into my pussy, licking it as if his tongue worshiped every fold and crevice of my sweet spot. His juicy lips feasted on my clit, smacking, and slurping. I couldn't stop moaning if I tried.

"Oooh! Ooh, oh-oh my God!" I stuttered while covering my face with my hands.

I felt the warm, wet puddle flooding the sheets underneath me as Kas flicked my pink pearl with his long tongue. I sat up on my elbows and marveled at the sight of him in between my thighs. Kas had a tongue that had been handcrafted by God himself. He could not be outdone, and he would not be outworked.

My eyes rolled toward the back of my head. “Oh my God, Kas! You’re gonna make me cummmm.”

He pulled away to look down at his dick that had turned brick in his pants, before glancing back up at me.

“You ready for me to show you how much he missed you?”

I nodded before eyeing his dick as his pants fell to his ankles. He looked me in my eyes while embedding himself between my thighs and pushing deep into the heart of my femininity.

My mouth gaped open, and a moan escaped from my lips. “Mmm, shit.”

His chiseled brown abs flexed as he curved his torso forward and wrapped his hand around my throat. “Goddamn, I missed you,” he growled under his breath.

He filled me up, each slow, deep stroke leaving my pussy weeping and me desperately moaning for more. Kas had a hold on me that no one else did, physically and spiritually. He lifted my legs onto his shoulders, allowing him to bury himself further into my depths.

“Oh my God, Kas, you feel so fuckin’ good,” I cried out, unable to stop myself from shouting to the rooftops. When we were done, I was sure Yara and all of our neighbors would know his name.

He folded my legs like a pretzel, pressing his palms into the back of my knees and thrusting forward. “Yeah, take this dick. Take every inch of this dick you missed, girl.” He snarled with the sexiest look in his eyes.

By the time we switched positions, my legs felt like Jell-O. I lay flat on my stomach as Kas dipped back inside of me from behind. Within seconds, he had my head hanging off the edge of the bed as he fucked me silly. After pulling me up on all fours, I twisted my neck to look back at him before sticking my tongue out to play with his.

“Tell me this is my pussy.” He growled in my ear while fucking the shit out of my womb.

I moaned while throwing my ass back against him. “It’s y-yours.” I purred.

"Mmm. It's all mine?"

"Y-yeah. A-all yours. It's all yours."

"Mmm, shit. Turn around and taste this dick."

Kas pulled out of me, and I spun around so my lips were right at his dick. He palmed the back of my head, forcing himself into the warmth of my mouth. "Oh fuck," he groaned.

His fingertips did figure-eights up and down my spine while I devoured as much of his length as I could. My fingers curved around his thickness before I spit on the head, lathering his long, brown rod with as much saliva as possible. I flashed my eyes up to see him sucking on his fingertips before curving forward and sliding a finger inside my asshole. I jerked forward, sucking harder and faster as he fucked the back of my throat until we were both satisfied.

* * *

I LAY THERE, my mind trapped in euphoric bliss while my body was wrapped in nothing but my sheets and Kasim's warm oak-brown arms. "You sure we can't just say fuck everything and everyone and run off together?" I quizzed before placing a kiss on his chest.

A long sigh escaped his lips. "I wish it were that simple, but this is all bigger than our emotions. I'm talking years, decades of alliances even. I can't ruin that for—"

"For what? Me? Is that what you were going to say?" I asked, sitting up on my elbows.

"Jrue, lay back down."

"No. Tell me what you were going to say first," I said defensively.

He huffed. "I thought you were okay with this."

A frown creased my face. "*Okay* with this? Is that what you thought just because I swallowed your kids, Kas? I'm a lot of fuckin' things right now. I'm surprised. Hurt. Jealous. Confused. But what I'm not is okay with this," I confirmed.

"Jrue—"

"No! You got to speak your peace about this, but I didn't!"

"Okay, so say whatever you gotta say. Get it off your chest," he insisted.

"I don't understand how you can want me so badly, but yet you're still going to stand at an altar and marry another woman willingly."

"I told you I know how crazy all of this shit sounds, but I can't fight my feelings for you. I need you to know how much I want you, Jrue. I tried to stop myself. I tried to quit you. But I can't. Why can't you understand that?"

"You want me, but you don't want *us*. That's what I don't understand!"

"Jrue."

"I think you should go," I told him before throwing on some clothes.

"Jrue."

"Whatever this is or isn't, it's done. I'm done."

"Jrue!"

"I'm serious, Kas. I can't keep sticking to you like glue, knowing you're someone else's man. I know too much to play myself out like that. I can't do it."

"I told you I don't love her!"

"You don't love her, but you're going to fuck her and have babies with her and sleep next to her every night!"

"We only have to be legally married for six months, and then we can get an annulment!" he announced.

"So you expect me to be your side chick for six months until you can dissolve the shit you couldn't figure out how to get out of in the first place?"

"It doesn't have to be as complicated as you're making it. Everybody can win if you just listen!" He pleaded to deaf ears.

"Listen to what! You get a wife and a chick on the side! She gets a husband and a family, and what do I get? To spend the day after each major holiday with you? And God forbid I get pregnant! You'll see our kid once a month, and they get to grow up wondering why daddy lives with one family, and we live somewhere else. No! I don't care if it's six months or sixty years, I can't do it. By the end of the weekend, you'll be a married man. It doesn't matter if our hearts want a different outcome. This is just the way it is," I concluded.

Five

YARA

NATHAN SAT across the booth from me with his eyes glued to the menu in his butterscotch hands. The restaurant was upscale and had a Latin vibe, with Latin American décor and music. Neither of us had been before. It was one of the ones we'd talked about going to before his last deployment but hadn't gotten around to it until now. I nervously glanced around the intimate space. There were a few cocktail tables scattered between rows of booths and four-seater tables. The waiter approached us, sitting down two glasses of ice water on the table before introducing himself. I eagerly gulped it down, dissolving half the glass before he walked away with our orders scribbled on his notepad.

"You good, bae?" Nate asked.

I jerked my head forward. "Yup. Y-yeah."

He arched a questioning brow. "You sure?"

I sighed. As much as I wanted to pretend things were normal between us, my conscience knew we were far from it. The baby growing inside me was like a ticking time bomb. I cleared my throat before speaking. "Actually, I—I don't think I feel too good."

"What's wrong? You feel sick?"

I bobbed my head slowly. "Yeah. And I've got a headache. The longer we sit in here, the worse it gets."

"But you love Latin food. You think you're coming down with something?"

"I don't know. Maybe." I shrugged. "Can we just go find the waiter and get our food to go? I'm gonna go to the bathroom."

"You're gonna throw up?"

I bolted from the table, eyes frantically searching for the restroom. Once inside the stall, I hovered over the floating toilet to puke my guts out.

"Ew. Fuck. Fuck. Fuck. Ew!" I groaned.

If there was one thing I hated doing, tossing my cookies was at the top of the list. After washing my hands and splashing some cold water on my face to wipe my mouth, I headed back to the table to see Nathan and the waiter bagging up our food. A sigh of relief escaped my lips.

"You feelin' better?" he questioned as we made our way back to the car.

"A little."

He opened the passenger side door for me, and I climbed inside. "You think it's food poisoning or like a stomach bug?" he quizzed.

I kept my eyes focused on the road as I shrugged. "I don't know. I just wanna lay down."

He reached over to place his hand on my thigh. "Don't worry, bae. I'll take care of you when we get back to your spot. Get you all cuddled up underneath some blankets, make you some soup if you don't want the food we got, rub your feet... the whole nine."

I shifted my eyes to him. "You're too good to me."

"Anything for my future wifey."

My heart fluttered at the mere mention of our wedding. We still hadn't set a date. Anytime he asked, I dodged his questions like the Matrix. I could only handle putting out one fire at a time. And right now, the baby inside me was setting my life ablaze. But I knew I couldn't avoid him or the subject forever. Nathan was thoughtful, attentive when he was on land, and sweet. There was never a doubt in my mind that he wouldn't be a great husband or father one day. I just didn't know if he would be a great father to a baby that *wasn't* his.

"You know what would really make me feel better?" I asked.

"What's that?"

"You inside me."

His eyes darted over to me. "You sure you feelin' up to that?"

"I think I can muster up the energy."

It had been a minute since I'd had the real thing. I hadn't been in the mood to be near a dick, let alone see one standing at full attention, but I had to do what I had to do. A twenty-minute car ride and a shower later, Nate and I were wrapped in the sweet, hot steam underneath the covers.

"Mmm, shit. You feel so good, baby." I purred as he thrust deeper inside me.

"Yeah? You like that?"

I moaned. "Mmm. Keep fuckin' me. Just like that. Mmm, yeah! Nut in this pussy, baby. It's all yours."

Nate growled in my ear while he continued to hump me with the speed of a jackrabbit. "Mmm, shit. This pussy feels so good."

My fingertips combed through his head full of waves, before I drilled my palms into his shoulders to roll him onto his back. Once I climbed on top of him and was entirely in control, I started to wind my hips in slow circles.

I tossed my head back as he caressed my nipples. "Mmm, yeah. Smack my ass, baby. Get nasty," I commanded.

He gave my ass a gentle tap before leaning forward to suck on my nipples. I rolled my eyes and continued to pop my ass, thrusting forward harder to get him to cum as quickly as possible.

"You like it when I ride you, baby?" I whispered in his ear.

Nate caressed my naked body as I rocked back and forth against him, ass cheeks slapping against his hairy brown thighs. "Mmm, shit. I love you, Yara. I love this fuckin' pussy," he claimed.

"Mmm, Nate. I love you too."

"Fuck, I want you to have my fuckin' kids, baby." He groaned while I bounced up and down on his dick.

"Then cum inside me, baby. I love you. I love you so much." I purred.

Six

KAS

The wedding day

MY JAW TICKED as I straightened the bowtie that was already pulling at my neck and partially constricting my airway. There I was, less than an hour away from marrying another woman, and I still couldn't manage to separate my thoughts from Jrue. I meant everything I said to her the last time I saw her, but that didn't change the circumstances. The knuckles of someone's hand hit the door before Kamil walked through.

He hooked his arm around my shoulder. "You look good, ak. Never thought I'd see the day you'd be the man of the hour in a tux."

I scoffed while staring at our reflections in the mirror. "You and me both."

"How you feelin'?"

I twisted my neck to face him. "You want the truth, or do you want me to tell you what you and everybody else wanna hear?" I asked.

"I want the truth, nigga."

I sighed. "I can't do this shit."

His face screwed up. "The fuck you mean? You standin' here in a fuckin' tailored tuxedo minutes before your wedding, and now you wanna be on your *Runaway Bride* shit?"

Emotions were already running high. I didn't need him making me feel worse. "I don't want this, and I don't want her," I contested.

"Okay, nigga. You need to breathe, aight? And think. Breathe and think. Can you do that?" he asked.

There was another quick knock on the door before our father stepped inside, causing us to pause our conversation in the heat of the moment.

"It's going to be a beautiful day, boys. I can feel it." He greeted us.

Kamil and I shot our eyes at each other, silently exchanging looks to make sure the other stayed quiet about our prior discussion. "Sure is, Pa," he replied.

"How's Janessa's father? Have you heard anything since his surgery?" Pa asked.

"He's stable. Still recovering in the hospital," Kamil informed him.

"Good."

"Nessa said the first thing he told her when he woke up from surgery was a war was coming."

"He feels it, too, huh? Well, we're not going to talk about war or our enemies today. Today is about joining our families and strengthening our bonds."

"Yeah, Pa. About that, I—"

Before I could finish my sentence, he shot his hand up to silence me. "I'm getting a call. I gotta take this. I'll see you boys out there," he said before leaving almost as quickly as he came.

Kamil took one last look at me before following out behind him. With only thirty minutes remaining before our wedding, I raced from one side of my father's home to the other, to find Cena. My fist collided with the door where she and her bridesmaids were getting ready on the other side. The door creaked open, and I stepped inside.

"Hey, uh. Can we get a minute alone? To talk?"

Cena put down the diamond earring she was about to put in her ear and nodded. "Can you all give us a minute?" I stepped to the side, allowing them to move past me. "Got cold feet?" she asked when we were alone.

I looked at her without responding, allowing my silence to speak for me. When too much time passed, she spoke up again. "Kas."

"I'm sorry, Cena. But, I can't d—"

She shook her head. "No, Kas. No."

"Listen to me, Cena. You don't understand. This shit is bigger than me. I'm ready to walk away from it all. Everything."

"She's worth that much to you? Worth your seat on your father's throne? Worth starting a war over?"

I tipped my head in a nod. "She is."

She sighed. "Wow. I respect what you're trying to do in the name of love, but we both have to do what we have to do for our families, and I can't let your heart get in the way of that. You can't walk out on me. Not today. We're supposed to be seamless."

"Respectfully, I didn't come in here to ask your permission. I just wanted to let you know my intentions before I go speak to my father."

Once again, silence spread between us like wildfire. The tension was thicker than a slab of ice. I turned to walk toward the door when I heard her voice call out, barely above a whisper.

"I'm pregnant, Kasim."

My eyes bugged so far out that they almost fell out of my head altogether. I snapped my neck in her direction, confident I didn't hear what I thought I did. "What?"

"Please, Kasim. You can't walk out on me. I–I need you."

My mouth instantly ran dry, prompting me to lick my lips. My eyes searched the room for a vacant seat. Her news made me feel like I'd been sucker punched in the gut and gotten the wind knocked out of me. I found the nearest couch and sat down. Cena followed, gliding the train of her dress across the floor.

"Rewind. Hold up. You're gonna have to explain," I said finally.

"I'll tell you anything you want to know when we're on our honeymoon."

We stared at each other in a silent standoff. The more time we spent not saying shit, the more serious she got. "You're serious, aren't you?"

"As a heart attack. And since I'm one of the players in your game of hearts, it's my heart against yours right now. And since you're not the one standing here nauseous in a wedding dress, I win today."

I sighed. "There's gotta be another way to figure this out so that we both win. I can be with Jrue, and you can raise your baby with whoever you want."

"My child has a father, Kasim. And this marriage is how we win. At least for now, okay? We can move forward with the annulment in six months as planned, but you have to be standing there when I walk down that aisle. Please, Kas."

I'd always heard that marriage was about compromise, and Cena had made it clear before we said 'I do' that she would have her foot on everyone's neck when it came to her unborn baby, even mine. My heart was being tugged in all different directions. It felt like everyone wanted a fucking piece of me, and the one thing I wanted, I couldn't have.

* * *

I WAS STANDING at the end of the aisle when my nerves kicked in tenfold. Flower girls lined the long path with red rose petals just as soft music began to play. It was a song I'd never heard before. Canaan escorted Cena down the aisle in place of their father. A part of her looked like she didn't want anything to do with him, while another looked like if he hadn't been there to hold her up, she'd faint. We locked eyes for a moment, knowing that we weren't the love of each other's lives or one another's forever. I watched everyone watching her as she inched further down the aisle, getting closer until we were standing side by side.

"Dearly beloved," the minister stated, "we are gathered here today to witness this man and this woman joining in holy matrimony."

Knees locked, I stood beside my bride, completely zoned out. We exchanged traditional vows, repeating after the minister that we would be faithful to one another in good times and bad; promising that we would love and cherish each other for as long as we both shall live. It was all bullshit. I took her shaking hand in mine, holding it steady as I slid the gold band on her finger. Cena's sad eyes prickled with tears as she returned the gesture.

The room fell silent when the minister asked if there were any objections to the marriage. I stood there wishing Jrue would burst in and stop the entire thing. I assumed there was a part of Cena that wished the same about whoever she'd been fuckin'.

"With the powers vested in me by the state of Pennsylvania, I now pronounce you Mr. and Mrs. Kasim Barnes. You may kiss your bride," he announced.

Cena's eyes took mine. We were both hesitant to move for the first few seconds before I leaned in and kissed her softly on the cheek. The room filled with applause from our guests, but I barely noticed. I was officially a married man, and my full attention still rested on Jrue.

Seven

YARA

Thirty minutes before the ceremony

"YARA, are the flower centerpieces on each table in the reception area?" Blake's unnerving voice rang through my earpiece.

I pulled my free ear away from the bridal suite door, careful not to make a sound before stepping away and answering. "Yes."

"You're sure?"

"Positive. I just came from the area not too long ago and checked myself. I was just about to go into the bridal suite and check on the bride, but she's... occupied."

"What do you mean occupied?"

"She's having a private conversation... with the groom. I didn't want to interrupt."

Blake sighed. "Okay. Let me know if they aren't out of there in fifteen."

"Yup."

I yawned as my heels clicked against the marble floor in the foyer, passing by the hundreds of red roses adorning the grand staircase. The new last-minute wedding venue was Cena's soon-to-be father-in-law's mansion. We'd been working since before the sun came up, preparing for the big day, ensuring every T had been crossed and every table linen had been steamed. Had it not been for Blake's unwelcomed interruption, I would still be trying to pick my mouth up off the ground. I couldn't believe Cena was pregnant. The tea was piping hot and dying to be spilled, but I didn't know whether to tell Jrue. She was already hurting over him, and I knew that kind of news would be the icing on her brokenhearted cake.

Aside from that, I'd been dreading having to be in the same room as Canaan. To think, sometimes just looking at him used to make my pussy cry. My body used to crave his touch, and now I wouldn't touch him with a ten-foot pole. I walked over to swipe a fallen rose petal off the floor from the floral arrangement on the grand piano lid.

"The guests have all been seated. Let's start getting the wedding party ready," Blake announced.

"Yeah, okay."

Thirty minutes later, Cena walked down the aisle and said 'I do' to the man my best friend loved. Everything about their entire wedding was breathtaking, and I couldn't help but hate every minute of it.

* * *

OVERSIZED BOUQUETS of bright red roses imported from Italy christened the center of each round table, while black ribbon decorated the backs of the Chiavari chairs. Servers hustled and bustled through the sea of dressed-up guests with trays filled with greasy appetizers and bubbling champagne. You could smell the wealth in the room. I glanced over at the mountain of gifts and envelopes on the gift table and then at the wedding cake. With six tiers, it was too beautiful and damn sure too expensive to slice into.

The DJ announced the wedding party, and I darted my eyes away when he said Canaan's name, but not before seeing the tips of his middle finger and thumb kissing to form the letter O as he held it over his heart. The crowd whistled and cheered when Mr. and Mrs. Kasim Barnes were announced. I could've slipped into a hole in the floor. Ice tinkled in the glass of my ice-cold water as I scanned the room, eyeing the bride and groom as they shared their first dance. I didn't know if it was the baby or the sight of them that made my stomach turn, but somehow, I couldn't pry my daggering eyes away.

"Yara, go around and make sure all the candles on the tables are still lit," Blake instructed via my earpiece.

"On it," I responded before setting my glass of water down by the bar.

Light on my feet, I buzzed through the room as the live band played and photographers flashed and snapped every few seconds. All I wanted to do was kick off my shoes and grab a stiff drink from the bar, but that wasn't possible. The only thing that brought a partial smile to my face was pretending the glasses of water I'd been sipping all day were vodka. After relighting the floating candles around a few centerpieces, I heard Canaan's familiar voice call out from behind me, booming over the loud music. "Yara?" I froze in place, unwilling to move until he spoke a second time. "What, you can't speak now?"

I slowly spun around on my heels to face him. "The last time you hit my phone, you were on one."

"Again, I'm sorry about that."

"Mmhm."

I eyed him closely. As much as I hated to admit it, he looked good. It was my first time seeing him in a tux, and he certainly didn't disappoint.

"How you been? It's been a lil minute."

"I guess it has."

"You're the last person I expected to see around this jawn."

"Well, surprise," I stated dryly.

"Well, since you are here, what's up? You drinkin'?" he asked, offering me a glass of champagne from a nearby tray.

I shook my head. "No. I'm working. I'm your sister's wedding planner."

"C'mon, even you can let loose for a minute. Besides, she won't care. The wedding is over now. Take a shot with me."

"My boss will care. And, no, Canaan, I can't."

"Can't or won't?" he quizzed, arching his brow.

"Can't," I repeated, eyes avoiding his gaze.

He stepped closer to me. "Why you actin' like that?"

"I'm not acting like anything. I told you I'm working. Maybe I'll snag a piece of that expensive ass cake before I go."

"Mmhm. You sure there isn't something you need to tell me?"

I folded my arms across my chest, losing my control over my attitude. "I could be asking you the same thing."

He scoffed. "What the fuck does that mean?"

"You know exactly what it means."

"Nah, I don't."

"You know what, we shouldn't be having this conversation here," I stated before trying to walk away.

He stepped in front of me, blocking my path. "Nah, I think we should."

"Trust me. You don't wanna take it there with me right now."

I darted past him, trekking toward the hallway when he cornered me again. "What the hell is your problem, Yara?"

"My problem is that you're a liar! Why the hell did you lie to me and tell me your last name was Mitchell when we met?"

"Why does that shit matter now?"

"Because it does! I know we didn't tell each other every fuckin' thing, but lying about your name—that's childish. I only found out because I just happened to be on the team planning and executing your sister's wedding!"

"What do you want me to do? You know now, and what did it change? Nothing."

I scoffed. "Yeah, well, I wish it did."

"There you go dreamin' again," he stated, his brown orbs rolling toward the ceiling.

"No, nigga! You're the one who wants a dream! You wanna do whatever you wanna do when you wanna do it, and you just want everyone else to fall in line!"

His brow creased. "Where is all this extra hormonal shit coming from, Yara? If I didn't know any better, I'd say you sound—" He paused. "Hold up. Are–are you pregnant?"

"Don't change the subject. We're not talking about me. We're talking about you!"

"Answer my question!"

"That's none of your business!"

"Bullshit! Tell me the truth, Yara. Are you pregnant or not?"

"What if I am? You said it yourself; it doesn't change shit."

His brows snapped. "Why the fuck didn't you tell me?"

"Because there's nothing to tell! I can handle it."

"Is that because it's not mine?" His question made me go silent. "Yara. Answer me," he demanded.

"It's yours, Canaan."

His eyes went cold. "Are you fuckin' serious?"

"Yes."

"How far along are you?"

"I—I don't know. I haven't been to the doctor yet."

"So you don't know for sure if you are or not."

"I took the test, Canaan. I'm pregnant, but don't worry about it. I told you, I'll handle it."

"You damn right you will because this wasn't a part of our fuckin' arrangement, Yara! Goddammit, man! Shit! I don't need this shit right now, yo."

My forehead wrinkled. "You think I do? I'm not the one that wanted to get into this. You did!" I accused before storming off.

One fully clothed conversation with him, and I was pissed the hell off. It became exasperatingly clear that we were more compatible when we were naked. I swiped the burning tears from my eyes and shoved my repulsive thoughts of him back down my throat before continuing to make my way around to ensure everything about the wedding day from hell was still flowing smoothly.

Eight

JRUE

SATURDAY NIGHT ROLLED AROUND, and I'd gotten consumed with researching genetics and family ancestry. I was still toying around with the idea of getting a blood test done, when Yara came through the front door.

"Hey." She huffed.

"Hey. How was it?" I asked.

Her brows sloped. "You sure you really wanna know?"

I huffed while closing my laptop. "Yeah. I can take it."

"Well, they are officially married."

My shoulders sank. "Oh."

"I'm sorry, girl. I swear I am, but for what it's worth, he wanted to run, Jrue."

"How do you know that?"

She sighed before making her way into the living room. "I overheard them talking before the ceremony."

"What did he say?"

"He told her that he wanted to walk away from it all. He said that you were worth starting a war over, even though I don't know what that meant. But then, she, uh—well, I don't know that I should tell you the rest. I don't wanna add insult to injury."

"Just say it!"

"She told him she was pregnant, Jrue."

I blinked rapidly, trying to process what I'd just heard. "S–she what?"

"I know. I know. I'm so sorry, girl. I've been going back and forth on whether or not to say anything. I know that nigga did a number on your heart."

"I just don't... get it. He told me he didn't love her. That he only wanted me," I recalled while shaking my head. "I was a fuckin' fool."

"Hey, just know that no matter how long it takes you to get over this nigga, I'll be right here in the trenches with you," she assured me.

"Thanks, girl. I can't believe I thought he was the one, Ya-Ya. I'm beginning to think the right nigga is, like, a figment of my imagination or something."

"You might be right about that, girl. And hey, if it's any consolation, Canaan clocked me on the pregnancy tonight."

My brows raised as I patted my cheeks. "Damn. How'd he take the news?"

She smacked her cherry red painted lips. "Dumb, just like I thought he would."

"What did he say?"

"Asked if it was his and how far along I was. I told him I hadn't been to the doctor yet. He said, and I quote, that he '*didn't need this shit right now*' and that this '*wasn't a part of our fuckin' arrangement,*'" she said with air quotes.

"And what did you say back?"

"I told him I would handle it."

"How do you plan to do that?"

She looked at me flatly before folding her arms across her chest. "I don't know."

"Sheesh. For something that was supposed to be light, it sure is sounding *real* heavy," I stated.

"Tell me about it. I feel like I have the weight of the world on my fuckin' shoulders right now."

A breath rushed out with a quick sigh. "Not to be a pessimist or add more stress to your plate, but when *are* you planning to go to the doctor?"

She swiped her fingertips across her eyelids, which were dampening by the second. Then she let out a shaky sigh. "Listen, I'm, um, still formulating my plan, okay? Trying to figure out what I want out of this, you know? Just know that I got this. I got me."

I outstretched my arms to her, awaiting a comforting hug. "I believe you, girl," I assured her with a small smile, "and I got you too."

Her eyebrows drew together before she allowed herself to fall into my arms and hug me back. The downward spiral our lives seemed to be in had both of us feeling a little misty. After a few seconds of silent consoling, she pulled away.

Yara's lungs discharged a grunted breath. "I'm going to go shower off this long ass, exhausting ass day and sleep until noon tomorrow," she declared. "Only wake me if the house is on fire, aight?"

"Yup. Got it."

* * *

THE NEWS of Kas becoming a husband and a father in the same day didn't fully sink in until forty-five minutes later. And when it did, it crashed into me like a tidal wave. The thought of calling and cussing him out on his wedding day crossed my mind a time or two, but whenever I picked up the phone, I tossed it back down a minute later. I felt betrayed. Lied to. Even taken advantage of. What was the point of saying all that shit to me about his feelings and how much he wanted me if he had been sleeping with *his wife* all along?

I ejected a tight-lipped huff. "Heartless dickhead."

He tried to make me sound crazy for tossing him out of my spot when I told him I didn't want to be his secret and that I couldn't play myself out like that. The *nerve* of that nigga to think he was about to keep getting my cake when he'd already put a bun in her oven. My eyes darted to my sheets, and the instant replays of our final romp began to take over my thoughts. My face twinged with heat as I jumped up and started to strip the bed and toss everything in the washing machine. I no longer wanted the traces of his scent trapped in my sheets. He was married, becoming a father, and dead to me.

The more I stewed in my feelings, the more I realized that Yara was settling down. Kas had settled. And I just seemed to be hanging in the balance. I thought our story was still being written, but his marriage and unborn baby had placed a giant period at the end of our messy, consuming, ridiculous, run-on sentence of a relationship. I had no other choice but to file away my feelings for him once and for all.

After changing my sheets and taking a shower, I crawled into bed and started checking my emails. My eyes widened when I opened a message from a potential client.

Jrue,

My name is Unique Harris, and I am reaching out on behalf of celebrity chef Lori Knight. She came across your work via your Instagram profile and fell in love! She is looking for an interior designer for her new restaurant that will be opening in the Bay Area next year and would like to know if you are willing to travel. Of course, all fees will be paid. Please get back to me at your earliest convenience on when you'd be able to set up a call and discuss things further to see if it would be a good fit.

I look forward to hearing from you soon,

Unique Harris
Executive Assistant for Chef Lori Knight

My heart skipped a beat as my eyes glazed over the email three more times. Getting buzz and booking paid clients around the city was dope, but potentially becoming a designer for a celebrity was on a whole other level. A half smile lifted the right side of my lips. It was the first time I felt like I was coming into my own and the world was embracing my talent. My career was on the fast track, and although I didn't have anyone to celebrate with, I finally had a reason to smile again.

Nine

CANAAN

IT HAD BEEN a few days since the wedding, and the news of Yara's pregnancy still had my head spinning. I'd been busy running my father's business operations while Cena was off on her honeymoon, but concentrating was almost impossible, knowing Yara was carrying my baby and Trinity was wearing my ring. I knew I couldn't let anyone find out, especially Trinity. She'd been sending me apartments to look at around the city every other day, anxious to start living the life she should've been five years ago.

The first business matter I was hit with the moment I opened my eyes was the news that a few shipments of drugs were missing. I knew it was going to cost us, and it was a mistake that I was going to have to slide a nigga for. Frustration coursed through my veins as I worked to track down the missing drugs.

"How many shipments are missing?" I asked one of my father's soldiers.

"Three," he confirmed.

"Who was responsible for the pickup?"

"Javier and Lamarcus."

"Bet. Find 'em and let me know when you do. I want to handle them myself."

"You sure?"

"I'm positive."

I ended the call, anxious to release my pent-up aggression by wiping a nigga out. With all the pressure on my shoulders, I couldn't wait to kill. I'd always known I was fucked up. A ruthless and selfish mothafucka with a thirst for power and pain. There had been a darkness inside me for as far back as I could remember. I figured it was why my father took me under his wing and trained me to be the killer I was, especially regarding my family and my money.

Two hours later, I had them both on their knees with my finger itching to pull the trigger. I didn't ask questions or ask for reasoning as to why they tried to steal from my family. I didn't give a fuck.

"All the fuck you niggas had to do was be loyal." I barked at them, disappointment laced in my tone.

They didn't even bother trying to make up excuses because they knew even the best one wouldn't save them. Besides, I was in charge, and I had to make an example out of niggas who went against me. When my money and reputation were on the table, they would either pay with cold, hard cash or their lives. I let my gun sing without care or concern, watching the bullets fly and their bodies hit the ground.

* * *

AFTER A MUCH-NEEDED SHOWER AND A BLUNT, I picked up my phone to hit up Yara. The phone rang twice before she sent me to voicemail. I called two more times before she texted me.

Yara: *Stop calling me.*
Me: *We need to talk.*
Yara: *You made it clear we don't have shit to discuss.*
Me: *Look, all you gotta do is handle it. I'll pay for whatever.*
Yara: *I don't need your money. I'm good.*
Me: *Let me know when it's taken care of.*
Yara: *Nigga, fuck you! Don't ever hit my phone again!*

Before I had the chance to respond, Julius called. I stared at the screen for a few seconds, drawing a deep breath.

"Boss," I answered.

"I've got a meeting set for tonight with all the family heads. Are you ready?"

A slow smile crept across my face as I dipped my chin in a quick nod. "I was born ready," I assured him.

"Meet me at my house in an hour."

"Bet," I replied before ending the call.

While Cena was off on her honeymoon, Julius worked to call a special meeting with all the family heads in The Order to vote me in as the permanent head of the McQueen family. By the time my sister stepped foot back on American soil, I would be in charge, and there wouldn't be shit she could do about it.

An hour later, I whizzed up his long driveway, noticing no other cars, and started feeling unsettled. I made my way through the doors of Julius's study and took a seat.

"Where's everyone?"

"I wanted you here early to talk."

"About?"

"I want to know how much you know about your father's gambling debts and his deal with the Riveras to pay them off?"

My brows raised. "You know about his deal with the Riveras?"

"I do. What I don't know is why he went behind my back and did it. Do you?"

"He said it was a backup deal," I answered.

"How long did you know?"

"He told me the night he died. The night I—" I paused. "He said that he made it just in case Cena and Kas didn't get married, but they did, so it's dead, right?"

"Your marriage to Layla Rivera may be off, but his debts are still very much on the table. And now that he's gone, those debts are yours as the new head of the McQueen family. That is if heading your family is still what you want."

I kept my poker face up for as long as I could, but I was seething on the inside. Even from the grave, my father and his gambling addiction were haunting me. I had enough shit on my plate. I didn't need niggas from New York and Connecticut on my ass too. I needed to confirm my seat at the head of the McQueen table and the protection that came with it.

I released a tight breath as my eyes narrowed. "Of course, it's what I want. It's my birthright!" I asserted, inflating my chest with a deep breath.

"Don't worry. I'll help you get Ruiz under control. You can handle him."

I shifted uncomfortably in my seat before responding. "My father said he considered you a friend because of your business dealings, but he didn't trust you. Why should I?"

"What did your father tell you was in the deal for you if you married Ruiz's daughter?" he asked, answering my question with one of his own.

I cleared my throat before deciding to spill my father's secret from beyond the grave. "Uh, he told me that I would oversee the day-to-day operations in their new casinos—"

"*New* casinos?" he interrupted.

"Yeah," I answered. "They would be building here... on our territory."

Julius's furrowed brows raised before he nodded. I watched him roll his tongue across his teeth as if he were debating what to say next. "He considered me a friend because we did business together but told you he didn't trust me. Yet, our arrangement *was* a business deal, and he was going to leave me with *nothing*. I expected as much from him to do that to me, but his own son?"

"What do you mean?" I quizzed, my heart rate escalating by the second.

Air eased from his lungs before he addressed my question. "I hate to break it to you, but there was never a leadership position for you there because that deal was never going to go through on land that *I* own."

"What? Are you sayin' he lied to me? And what do you mean land that you own?"

"I'm afraid so, Canaan. To help your father out with his debt, I arranged a cut of his land for myself to run how I see fit. As soon as the ink dried on my son's marriage certificate, it became mine. Your father can't lease something that isn't his."

My fist tightened. "How much did he give you?"

"A third."

"A fuckin'—" I paused, careful of my tone. "A third?"

"Big debts require big sacrifices. I've spoken with Ruiz, and we've agreed on some new terms discussed one-on-one. And he's agreed to give you his vote tonight."

A long sigh of relief eased out of my nostrils. "Thank you."

"God bless the dead, but now I guess you can decide for yourself which one of us is more trustworthy."

Forty-five minutes later, I was officially voted in as the head of the McQueen family, with all rights and privileges. A smile stretched across my face. I was officially in the mothafuckin driver's seat.

Ten

KAS

Sitges, Barcelona, Spain

CENA and I had been away on our honeymoon for two days in a city known for having three hundred days of sun each year. We were tucked away in a fifteenth-century Catalan villa near the sea with impressive views of the hills and vineyards around us. With over ten bedrooms, two private patios, a four-sided infinity pool, and various private terraces and sitting areas, we didn't have a problem staying out of each other's way. Besides, we were too jetlagged to do anything but eat and sleep the first day, barely speaking except in passing.

The sun's rays were set to a cozy seventy-three degrees, and a breeze whistled through the palm trees that shaded the infinity pool. I sat outside on the private terrace, scrolling through Jrue's Instagram feed to see what she'd been up to. She hadn't posted anything new since the mixer, not even a story. It amazed me how sick I still was over her. I'd never been strung up in my feelings over a female before. As much as I stood on my word, I was ready to turn back on it all for Jrue.

My eyes traveled through the window, spotting Cena making her way into the full gourmet kitchen. I watched her for a few seconds, debating whether to approach her. She was one of the reasons, amongst many, why Jrue and I couldn't be together. Never mind what or who I wanted. I stood to my feet and proceeded through the wooden French doors leading back inside, ready to get to the bottom of her secrets, the first being who the father of her unborn child was.

Cena was standing at the oversized island with her eyes pinned to the menu to see what the private chef would prepare for the day when I spoke. "Hey."

"Kasim, hey..."

"Did you sleep well?"

"How'd you sleep?"

We asked each other simultaneously, jumbling our sentences together before sharing a quiet laugh.

"I'm sorry. You go first," I told her.

"I was asking, did you sleep well?"

"Yeah. You?"

"Yeah."

She grabbed a few fresh strawberries and grapes from the bowl of fresh fruit on the counter. There was a bottle of champagne in a pool of melted ice and two glasses with a note card that read *Congratulazioni, Mr. e Mrs. Barnes* inside.

"It's real now, huh?" she asked, eyeing me from across the kitchen island.

I sighed before rubbing the back of my neck. "Coming to terms with this shit is hard," I admitted.

"I know. And listen, I know you have a lot of questions."

"You damn right I do."

"So go ahead," she offered before propping herself up on the counter, "ask me anything."

"Anything?"

She shrugged. "Sure. What's a little deep, dark confession amongst friends? Besides, we're at the edge of the village, and this is a very private space. We can speak as freely as we want to here, Kasim. I promise you that."

I eyed her closely. "You've been here before?"

"Once."

"With him?"

"Yes."

"Who is he, Cena?"

"His name is Liam Morgan. He's my father's business attorney. He helps set up different businesses for our family."

"Liam? That nigga sounds white."

"He is..." she confessed before tearing her eyes away from me and refocusing them on the dining room adjacent to the kitchen.

"Does he know what your family does? And about The Order?"

"Yes, he does."

"How long has this been a thing?"

"Almost two years," she answered.

My brows jutted up, wrinkling my forehead. "So you'd been dealing with him before you were supposed to marry my brother?"

"Yes, Kasim."

"When did you find out you were pregnant?"

"A few months ago."

"A few months ago? How far along are you?"

"A little over four months," she confessed. "And it's a boy."

"So, had Koda not gotten killed, and he was standing here in my place right now, you would've used him to clean up your mess like you're using me?"

"I'm not using you, Kasim. We're allies who are helping each other."

"Helping each other? It's been fuck what I've wanted from the start of this entire situation, Cena! I feel like I'm being used as a pawn in everybody's fuckin' game!" I yelled, my voice echoing through the villa.

"I'm sorry you feel that way," she said calmly, "but you're not a pawn to me. You're all I have. We had to go through with it, Kasim. It was the only way. I can't risk anyone finding out about Liam or my son until I can officially take over as the head of my family. Once I'm in the driver's seat, I'll be able to do things how I want and make my own rules and business arrangements. All you have to do is stay married to me for six months. Six months is all I'm asking you for. Please," she begged.

I paused for a few seconds to settle my mind and align my thoughts. "So you'd deliver while we were married?"

She nodded. "Yes."

"And you want everyone to think that the baby you're carrying is mine?"

"Once we dissolve the marriage, we can go our separate ways. I'll be with Liam, and we'll raise *our* son together, the way it should've been all along."

I scoffed. "And what about me? And what about your unpredictable ass brother, since you got a plan for everything?"

"Canaan and I have a meeting with our father's executor next week to settle his estate. He'll get a copy of the will with my father's intentions written out, and I'll get mine. It'll all be there in black and white. I don't want any arguments over this shit."

"And after that?"

"I plan to call a meeting with the family heads and make it official. Once it is, things will start to settle down. Trust me."

I scoffed. "Trust you? That's a strong statement."

"I'm trying my best to be fair here."

I scoffed. She was throwing out one triggering word after another. I didn't trust a soul outside my brothers, and shit hadn't been fair since Koda was killed. "You really don't know shit if you think any of this is fair!"

Cena narrowed her honey-brown eyes at me. "You think I don't understand what's fair and what's not? Liam is the keeper of my secrets. He's my rock. He's my village. I want to raise this baby with him out loud, but… I'm sitting here married to you."

I glanced at her. "You're okay with someone having that much power over you?"

"When it feels this good, yeah."

"Mmm."

"Is that not how you feel about… your girl?"

"This feeling shit is new to me. I don't know how I feel half the time."

"Might I remind you that you were ready and willing to walk away from me on our wedding day for her? If that's not power, then I don't know what is."

I ran my hand down my beard. "Yeah, well, all that's over now."

"You can still have the life you want with the person you want to have it with, Kasim. I'm not stopping you."

I wagged my head from left to right. "Nah. She made it clear she don't want shit to do with me if I'm married to you."

"Six months isn't a life sentence."

My shoulders rose and fell. "Feels like it."

"I mean, if you insist on looking at our marriage as a prison sentence, then welcome to day two of your 180-day sentence. Only 178 more days to go."

I smacked my teeth. "Shut up, yo."

"I'm just saying, is it really that long to wait if you know the one you love will be standing there on the other side of it?"

"How do I know she'll be there?"

"If she isn't, then you go find her and tell her how you feel. As complicated as y'all niggas make us sound, we're not. All we ask for is loyalty, understanding, honesty... I mean, stop me any time here."

"Aight, aight. Chill. I get it."

"She doesn't need some over-the-top grand gesture to know how you feel. I mean, that's cool and all, but all you have to do is get her to listen and tell her how you feel when she's all ears."

"Damn. Talkin' to you makes me wish I had a sister growing up instead of two knuckle-headed brothers."

"You should expect nothing less than good listening skills and advice from a Scorpio," she boasted.

My forehead creased. "Hold up. You part of the Scorpio gang too?"

"Hell yeah! October thirty-first! Gang, gang!" she joked.

"Your birthday is on Halloween?" I asked, instantly thinking of Jrue.

"Yeah. Canaan and I were Halloween babies. That's probably why that nigga's so deranged, for real."

I huffed out a quick laugh. "You might be right about that shit."

"You have no idea. Growing up with Canaan was so hard, yo. I swear, he *always* felt like he had to prove himself to be better than me. Like, it was some unspoken competition. He wanted power for the sake of having power. We didn't have the twin intuition shit you hear about. I figured it was because he was a boy and I was a girl, but no. We're just twins that don't click. What about you and your brothers? Were y'all close?" she asked, looking for a window into my past.

"Yeah. I mean, well, I'm the middle child, so I could run with Koda or Kamil. But Kamil, that's my ace, y'know? We're three years apart but always closer than Koda and me."

"Brotherly competition?"

I shook my head. "Nah, it wasn't nothin' like that. I don't know if it was ego, or our personalities simply didn't mesh. Kamil is more light-hearted and a jokester. Koda was always so stern and reserved."

"And what about you? What are you?"

"Maybe a little bit of both. Maybe neither. I don't know. Guess it just depends on the day or the situation."

"Or the person," she suggested.

"Yeah. That too."

I shook my head. "What?" she asked.

"Nothing."

"You already startin' off the marriage with lies, Kasim?" she joked. "I sat here and told you my deepest, darkest secret of all time!"

"Fine, aight. Chill. So, you remember the day she ran into us at the restaurant, and I ran out after her?"

She dipped her chin in agreement. "Yeah."

"Well, to try and win her back, or at least get her to talk to me, I made her a mixtape."

"Hold up. A what?" Cena chuckled.

"Before you go and start callin' me a corny nigga, hear me out. Once we were at a carnival and shit, and she said somethin' like if the love ain't feel like nineties R&B, she ain't want it. We joked about it and shit at the time, but when everything got bad, I turned to the music."

"Did it work?"

"Yeah. We talked."

"Did you tell her about our families and us?"

I nodded. "I did."

"And she didn't run away screaming?"

"Nah. She ain't like that. Jrue's... I don't know. She's different. She's a vibe I've never felt before. Like, she's so creative. Her shit is on another wavelength, for real." Cena interrupted me with a chuckle. "What?"

"Nothing. It's cute, that's all."

"What's cute?"

"This is the first time I think I've ever seen you smile. It's her. She brings out this light in you, pushing back all your darkness. And with our families, you know there's a lot of darkness."

"Is it weird that you kind of remind her in some ways?"

"How?" she inquired.

"Your independence and wit. You're easy to talk to like she is. I don't know. I feel like I can be myself around you. I ain't felt like that with nobody else but her."

Cena nodded. "Well, good. I don't want this marriage to be painful for either of us. You deserve to be happy, Kasim. We both do."

Before I had the chance to respond, my phone started to vibrate in my pocket. I tore my eyes away from her long enough to fish it out of my pocket and look at the screen. Kamil was calling. We were six hours ahead of Philly time, so it was two o'clock in the morning over there.

"Hello?" I answered.

"Yo, we gotta talk. Can you talk?"

My face turned to stone. "What's wrong?"

"There was a meeting with all the family heads in The Order. They voted Canaan McQueen in as the head of his family."

My eyes popped wide. "They what!" I yelled.

"What? What's wrong?" Cena asked, hopping down from the counter to make her way over to me.

Instead of responding, I put the phone on speaker. "Repeat what you said, Kamil."

"I said there was a meeting with all the family heads. They voted in Canaan McQueen as the new head of his family."

My eyes shot from the phone to Cena. A single tear slipped down her cheek. I knew she was afraid, not only for herself but for her son too.

"No! No! No! No! This wasn't supposed to happen! No! I told you my father wanted me to be the head of our family, not Canaan! We have to fix this. I have to fix this!" she yelled, pacing the kitchen floor.

"Cena, calm down!"

"I can't calm down! What about my life? What about my ba—"

Before she could answer, I hung up the phone on Kamil and went over to grab her shoulders to stop her from moving. She buried her head in my chest and sobbed for a few minutes. "I knew he would do this. I just didn't think he'd do it this soon," she mumbled.

"I'm sorry, Cena. Tell me what you wanna do. Do you want me to talk to my father?"

"No. I have to handle this myself right now. We have to go back home. I have to get back to Philly and fix this."

"How do you plan to fix this? They've already voted."

"And they can vote again! Once I have the proof of his wishes in my father's will, they'll have no choice!"

"You're going to need more than that, Cena. We both know that. But first, I need you to calm down. All this stressing and pacing ain't good for you or your son," I reminded her.

She drew in a pensive breath before slowly releasing it. "Y-you're right. Help me secure my father's seat, Kasim. Help me take down my brother and your father and secure their seats for ourselves. Then we can change things. We can rule this organization how we want to," she proposed.

I could see the desperation in her eyes. "Even if I agreed to do that, we need more on Canaan... a lot more. We have to prove he's unfit to make decisions for your father's organization. It was easy for them to vote him in for two reasons: One, you were out of the country, and two, he'd already been doing the day-to-day stuff when your father got sick. You were his queen, Cena. He was protecting you, but now, you gon' have to start movin' niggas off the board quickly."

Another long sigh etched from her lungs. "I need to think."

"Have the police questioned you anymore after the shooting at the funeral?" I asked.

"They did. They think the two could be connected somehow."

"So, they are actively pursuing this, which means they are watching all of us."

She nodded. "Yeah."

"Fuck." I grumbled.

"There's more I found out the night before the wedding... about the night my father was stabbed."

"What?"

"I talked to Lorraine, the night nurse that found my father. She mentioned she saw Canaan that night but didn't tell the police."

My brow creased. "Why would she leave that out?"

"I pulled the camera footage from that night and saw him leave."

"Did you see him come back?"

"No. There's no camera in my father's room or that entire corridor for privacy."

"What about a back entrance?"

"The camera was out."

I sighed. "So you have no way of knowing if it was him."

She shook her head. "No, but I wouldn't put it past him."

"Why the change of tune? At the hospital, you were sure he didn't have shit to do with it."

"You weren't in the limo with him the day of the funeral. He was aloof and unremorseful. It was as if he was playing a role. Just there for show, you know? And when it came time to go up to the casket, he didn't even look at him."

"Outside of your suspicions, what else is there? What else do you have?"

"Just give me some time, okay? I know there's more. I know I can find more."

"Okay. And I'll help you in whatever way I can, aight?"

"Thank you."

"I'll call a car to come and transport us to the airport."

"I'll go pack our bags," she stated before disappearing.

I knew a war against our families would begin the minute Cena and I stepped back on American soil. But if starting a war meant I got to be with Jrue, I was ready and willing to set all of Philly on fire.

Eleven

YARA

I SAT INSIDE MY CAR, staring at the ultrasound in the passenger seat. The doctor and the ultrasound confirmed that I was about nine weeks along. The confirmation left my head spinning on its axis. Everything was *real* and dreamlike at the same time: the pregnancy, the baby, all of it. I spent so many weeks convincing myself it was inaccurate, but there was no more running from the truth or hiding behind the great wall of denial I'd built.

"H-how the f-fuck did t-this ha-happen?" I whimpered through my tears. Canaan had been in my rearview for weeks, but he was still like an anchor holding me back.

I smeared the tears down my cheeks, knowing I was running out of time to decide. The thought of punching myself in the stomach or tossing a few pills down my throat to be done with it crossed my mind, but somehow, it was deeper than that to me. Growing up, family had always meant the world to me. But I recalled the financial pitfalls my parents had, trying to raise me. I also saw how much my cousin, Deja, struggled with having her son in her early twenties and raising him alone.

Hands shaking, I looked down at my phone to book an appointment at the abortion clinic. I'd debated the idea of abortion since the stick turned pink, tossing it to the back of my mind each time. Even with Jrue and Nate's feelings to consider, I'd never felt so alone. After all, it was my life. I was in the driver's seat. Everybody else was secondary, which meant I had to be in charge of my own decisions. I had to figure out what I wanted out of this since having a baby wasn't a part of my immediate plan.

I loved my job, but it was hectic and demanding. I already had to figure out how to balance being a career-driven woman while also learning how to be someone's wife. I didn't know if I was ready to tack on the emotional rollercoaster of motherhood to all of that. Besides, I didn't know if I could even be a good mother. With each passing thought, I picked the phone up and then placed it back in my lap. What would happen after I made the appointment? Would I back out at the last minute? Would I regret it if I went through it? Could I live with my decision? I needed more time to think, but the clock was ticking so loudly in my head that it was hard to hear anything else.

I snapped out of my thoughts when my phone rang. It was Nate. I tried to steady my breathing while clearing my throat before answering. "H-hey, bae."

"Hey. Where you at?"

"On the way, uh, home," I answered.

"Good. I'm headed down from Mom's house in Pittsburg to scoop you."

My brows snapped together in confusion. "Scoop me? For what?"

"I thought I'd surprise you with a romantic weekend getaway in New York."

"What? Are you for real?" I quizzed while sniffling.

"Yeah. Every woman is a romantic at heart, right? Ain't that what they say?" he asked, pushing out a soft chuckle.

"Yeah. I guess so."

"Well? Are you excited?"

"Yeah. I am. I mean, besides not knowing what to pack."

"According to my GPS, I've got another two hours to go, so you've got time to figure something out."

"Okay, cool."

Traveling from Philly to New York was about a two-hour drive, and with all the heavy shit weighing on my mind, I could use the quick escape to NYC for the weekend.

"Aight, I'll see you in a little bit."

"Drive safe. I love you."

"I love you, too."

"Oh, Nate! Wait."

"Yeah?"

A muted sigh escaped my lips. "There's, uh, something I need t-to, uh, to talk to you about when we get there," I stuttered.

"Is it serious?"

"We'll talk about it later," I promised.

"You sure?"

"Yeah. You said it yourself, I've gotta go figure out what I'm gonna wear, and you know perfection takes time," I stated with forced excitement.

* * *

LATER THAT EVENING, Nate and I were seated across from each other in a restaurant in the middle of Times Square.

"You good?" he asked.

"Yeah. Why?"

"I don't know. You seem jittery, like you've got a lot on your mind."

I had hoped to wait until we got to the dessert portion of our dinner before bringing it up, but my body language had other plans. "Uh, okay, well. I, uh–you, uh. You remember a few weeks ago when we went to that Latin restaurant for date night, and then we came home early and had that *amazing* sex?"

A smile walked up one side of his handsome face. "Hell yeah. How could I forget?"

"Do you remember what you said to me that night?"

"I said a lot of shit. We both did."

"I know. But y-you said one thing in particular."

"Refresh my memory, bae."

"You told me you wanted me to have your baby," I stated, hoping it would trigger his memory.

"Oh, yeah. I remember that."

"Did you mean it?"

His face went stern. "I put a ring on your finger, girl. Of course, I meant it."

I let out a breath I didn't know I'd been holding, allowing my lungs to kick back to life. "Good, because I—"

His lips squirmed to the side before he interrupted me. "Hold up. Are you trying to tell me what I think you're tellin' me?"

"I guess that depends on what you think I'm trying to say."

"Are you pregnant, baby?"

His voice was upbeat and joyous, bringing a grin to my lips. "Y-yeah. I am," I confessed.

"Are you for real?"

I dipped my chin in a quick nod. "Yeah. Are you mad?"

His bushy brown eyebrows shot up toward his hairline. "Mad? No. Surprised? Hell yeah. But it's in a good way."

Relief whooshed from my lungs. "Are you sure? I know neither of us was planning on a pregnancy, especially with just becoming engaged."

Instead of responding, Nate quickly left his seat to sit next to me. He slid his hand across my stomach. "It's going to be okay, Yara. I got us. All three of us," he assured me before kissing my forehead.

Happiness flattened my lungs as I looked into his warm, brown eyes. "How did I get so lucky to have you in my life?"

"You? I'm the lucky one, bae. Wow, yo. I can't believe I'm about to be a father. My mom is gonna flip when she finds out she's about to be a grandma."

"Can we, uh, not tell anyone right away? I just wanna keep things quiet for as long as we can. Is that okay?"

He tipped his head in a nod. "Yeah. I'm good with that."

"What do you think we should do about the wedding now?"

"You wanna move it up sooner than later or do something after you have the baby?"

My brows heightened. "Oh. Yeah. Wow. I hadn't thought about it. What do you want?"

"I'm good with whatever you wanna do."

I shrugged while glancing down at the ring on my finger. The diamonds were small but still glistened under the proper lighting. "Maybe we can wait and do something intimate after I have the baby? I think I like that idea."

"Cool."

I was relieved that Nate was receptive to the news of my pregnancy. I knew the minute the words fell off my lips, his reaction would help finalize my decision. I loved Nate with all my heart, and I was glad he was the man he was, the man I was going to marry. Maybe the baby was my chance for us to fall in love in a new way and would bring us even closer.

* * *

THE WEEKEND ROLLED BY, and Nate pulled up to my apartment on Sunday to drop me off. We'd spent the past few days getting lost in New York and checking out some of our favorite spots in the city. The baby and our wedding were our two most talked about topics. We'd gone from making it something intimate after I had the baby to a private elopement within the next few weeks.

"I hope you enjoyed yourself this weekend, baby."

"I had a great time, baby. That mini getaway was exactly what I needed."

"You want me to come up and kick it with you a lil longer before I hit the road?"

I shook my head. "No. Unless you're tired."

"Nah. I took an energy drink before we left New York, and I'm still pretty wired."

"What did I tell you about those things? They aren't good for you!"

"Relax. I don't drink them every day."

I rolled my eyes. "So you say."

"Anyway, I love you."

I kissed his lips. "I love you, too. Call me if you get tired."

"I will."

"You promise?" I quizzed, raising my right brow at him.

He bobbed his head. "Yeah."

"Okay."

I hopped out of the car and grabbed my overnight bag from the back seat before heading inside my building. I sailed through the door with a smile on my face when my eyes landed on Jrue. She was bobbing her head to Erykah Badu's "Tyrone" echoing from the Bluetooth speaker in the living room while cooking on the stove.

"Hey, girl, hey." I greeted her with a quick wave.

Instead of responding, she looked at me with the spatula held up to her lips and started singing. "I think you betta call Tyrone."

I laughed before joining in. "And tell him come on, help you get your shit," I continued.

Jrue laughed before turning the music down a few notches and then placing her attention back on the stove. "What's up? How was New York?"

"It was fun."

"What did you and hubby do?"

"We walked through Central Park yesterday morning, which was surprisingly nice. Kicked it in Times Square and caught a Broadway show Friday night."

"Mmm. Sounds fun."

"It was. But, uh, I-um, I told him. I-I told Nate," I stammered.

She whipped her neck back in my direction. "About the baby?"

"Yeah."

"And?"

"And, he was... happy about it."

I watched Jrue's dark brown eyebrows shoot up. "For real? Oh shit! That's great news!"

"And..."

"Wait, what?"

"We set a date."

"For the wedding? Oh my God! When is it?"

"Well, since we agreed to hold off on telling people about the pregnancy right away, we decided to push the wedding up. We're going to elope in a few weeks. Just the two of us," I announced.

Her facial expression went from excitement to a poker face as air blasted from her lungs. "Ya, I love you with all of my heart. You know that, right?"

"Yeah."

"So, when I say what I'm about to say, please know that it's coming from a good place."

I released a tight breath. "What is it?"

"You know that just because you're rushing to say *I do*, it doesn't guarantee a happy ending."

"Wait. You think I'm rushing? We've been together for years, Jrue! I always knew I was going to marry him. There's nothing new, rushed, or surprising about this!" I snapped.

"I'm not saying you shouldn't marry Nate. I think he's a great guy. I think he's good for you and good to you. I just—"

"What? Say it, Jrue!" I demanded.

She pushed out an exhale. "I just want you to make sure you know what you're getting into with this baby stuff. I mean, I'm glad he took the news well, but asking a man to raise another man's baby is a lot."

"That's why he doesn't know that it's not his baby," I alerted her.

Her eyes bugged. "What do you mean he *doesn't* know?"

"He asked if I was pregnant, and I told him yes, and he assumed it was his."

"And you didn't bother to correct him?"

I narrowed my eyes at her before smacking my lips. "I wouldn't have said shit to you if I knew you would judge me."

"I'm not trying to judge you. I'm just trying to get some clarity on what the hell your plan is because it sounds like you're trapping him."

"He's my fiancé, Jrue! He wants to be with me. No one is forcing him to marry me, unlike your man!" I yelled. The minute the words fell off my tongue, I regretted saying them. "Jrue, I'm sorry, I—"

She scoffed. "You what? Said exactly what was on your mind? Yeah, okay." Her eyes rolled skyward, and I knew she was doing her best to hold back her angry tears.

"I'm sorry, okay? I shouldn't have said that."

"Yeah, well, you did, so..."

She swiveled away from me to drain the excess grease from the pan and strain the spaghetti noodles, seemingly ignoring me altogether.

"Listen, I'm sorry. I don't know why I said that shit. I just felt like you were attacking me."

"How am I attacking you by asking you questions? You're defensive because I'm holding the mirror up to you and forcing you to face your shit, and you ain't brave enough to do it!"

Tears sprang out of my eyes. "How is it that you're the only one who can do no wrong, huh, Jrue?" I asked, arching an accusing brow.

She smacked her lips. "I don't know what you're talking about."

"Oh yeah? Well, let me give you an example. Kas."

Her dark brown brows snapped together in confusion. "Kas? What the fuck does he have to do with this?"

"It was one thing to fuck him when you didn't know he was engaged, but even after you knew, you still let him spin the block and hit it before his wedding. But you wanna talk about me fuckin' another nigga who ain't my man?"

"That's your problem, Ya-Ya! I never said shit about you fuckin' another nigga! All I said was it sounded like you were trappin' your nigga into fathering a kid that ain't his. If that's how you wanna handle *your* situation, then you do that, because it's *your* situation!" she spat.

"You're right. You're exactly right. It is my situation. And when I'm married in a few weeks, you won't have to worry about me comin' to you about my situation any fuckin' more!" I yelled before storming off to my room.

Twelve

JRUE

Two weeks later

I SHIFTED my weight from one leg to the other before moving forward half a step in the long-queued line at the airport security checkpoint. I was heading out to Los Angeles to meet with a potential celebrity client, and I was having a hard time being as excited about it as I wanted to be. For the past couple of weeks, Yara and I had become two ships passing in the night. If we weren't consumed by work and life, we simply stayed out of each other's way. We hadn't said more than a few words to each other since our blowout, and I wasn't pressing the issue. I had no say in her decisions for her life and her baby. Besides, I had been dealing with my own shit.

Charity and I had gotten the inside of our cheeks swabbed a few days ago, instead of doing a blood test, and were still waiting on the results. I'd spent so much time going back and forth about it and finally decided to go through with it at the last minute. I figured it was our best chance to see if our DNA results from the genealogy test were accurate or a fluke, but I'd been a jittery mess ever since.

I would have liked to blame my anxiety on my upcoming flight, but I knew better. Finding out if we were full-blood siblings, half, or not at all was a big step for us. A step that I didn't think we were ready for, especially if the results didn't turn out the way I hoped.

"Let's keep the line moving, people! Let's go! Let's go," the TSA officer hollered, trying to disperse people into different lines. We inched along until it was time to remove my shoes and toss my things in a couple of the plastic bins before walking through the body scanner. As soon as I slid my boots back on, I craned my neck to read the directional signs to my gate. After locating my gate, I had another forty-five minutes until my flight boarded, so I made my way to one of the small bars close by and pulled out my phone to see a text from my sister.

Charity: *Results are in. Check your email.*

Her text sent a hiccup to my heartbeat as I quickly scrolled to my email to open them. I shot up from my seat to find a quiet place to read and digest the results. Once inside the privacy of a handicapped bathroom stall, my eyes scanned the introductory text. *DNA testing was done to prove the siblingship of the alleged siblings, blah, blah. Based on testing results obtained by analyses, blah, blah, the probability of siblingship is 0%.*

My eyes froze on the screen. "Z-zero percent?"

My heart became a pattered mess, beating all out of cadence as I scrambled to call Charity. She answered on the third ring. "Did you look?" I asked, frantic.

"Yeah. I-I did."

"What does yours say, Charity?"

"What does yours say?"

Air emptied from my lungs. "Z-zero percent."

"Oh my God, mine too. Does that mean we're not—we're not—"

"No! Don't say it. This doesn't mean shit to me. It was stupid even to do this in the first place. I just—" I paused before sniffling. "I just can't believe I-I'm adopted."

"How do we know it's you and not me?"

I sucked in several deep breaths to calm myself before answering. "I was eight when you were born, Charity. I remember seeing her pregnant with you. Besides, we've seen Mom's old albums a million times. You have her bone structure and everything."

"I don't see it."

I huffed. "Yeah, okay. Wait. I'll send you a few pics I have on my phone. Let me know when you get them."

A few minutes passed before Charity spoke up. "I mean, I guess I see what you mean."

"Exactly, then look at me. No similarities to her or Dad outside of my complexion."

"I can't believe they lied to us for all these years!"

"Listen to me. I know you're mad. I'm mad, too. But don't say shit to Mom about this. I don't want her to know either of us knows, okay? Can you promise me that?"

She expelled a long sigh. "Okay, fine. I won't say anything. But even if I did, I don't care what some dumb ass test says, either. You're my sister. Period. And you're right. We never should've done it."

I sighed. "Where are you right now?"

"Down at the track. I had to break away from my friends for a bit for this shit. What about you?"

"Inside a bathroom at the fuckin' airport."

Charity laughed. "We're pathetic."

I sniffled before wiping my eyes. "I know, right."

"Wait, the airport? Where are you going?"

"I have a meeting with a celebrity chef in LA."

"Oh shit! Are you serious?"

"Yeah."

"Wow, Jrue! That's big!"

I smiled. "Thanks. With all this new clientele lined up at my door, who knows where it could take me."

"I'm proud of you, and I love you, Jrue."

"I love you, too."

"I should get back into school."

"Okay."

"Have a safe flight."

"Thanks. Bye."

* * *

THIRTY MINUTES LATER, we started the boarding process, and I took my seat in first class. Working with high-paid clientele was a vibe because had I been responsible for purchasing the cross-country flight, my ass would've *definitely* been in coach. I eased out a breath before relaxing my curls against the plush headrest. The last thing I did before closing my eyes was turn Beyonce's *Renaissance* album up a notch in my AirPods.

"We gon' fuck up the night," I echoed with my neck turned toward the window. We would be wheels up in a matter of minutes, and I would leave all my family drama and heartbreak in Philly. Moments later, I felt someone sit down in the seat beside mine and immediately cracked open my eyes to see who it was. He was a brown-skinned, bearded brotha with a fresh haircut. My heart gave a kick, and just like that, Kas was on my mind again.

"'Sup?" he asked.

I huffed. Even his voice sounded so similar to Kas's. "Hey."

Before he had a chance to spark a conversation, we were interrupted by the sound of the stewardess's voice. "Complimentary champagne?" she offered.

I smiled, knowing I could use a buzz, especially with the news I'd just gotten. "Yes, please."

The man beside me passed me a glass before taking one himself.

"I'm Demari," he announced himself.

I placed the glass up to my lips seconds before it was my turn to respond. "Mm, sorry. Jrue."

He cocked a half smile. "Nice to meet you. Is LAX your final destination?"

"Yeah. You?"

"Nah. Got a three-hour layover ahead of me before I head to Hawaii for a business conference."

"A work conference in Hawaii? Where do I sign up?" I asked with a soft laugh.

"What's taking you out to the west coast? Business or pleasure?"

"Business. A potential client is flying me out," I said before taking another sip of champagne.

"An all-expenses-paid trip? Where do I sign up?" he replied with a chuckle.

His lighthearted banter made me smile, so I kept Queen Bey on pause a little longer than I anticipated. "So, what do you do?"

"I'm in sales."

"What do you sell? And please, by all means, stop me if I'm being too nosy."

He shook his head. "Nah. You good. I work for a software company, so I'm responsible for negotiating contracts and giving presentations and demonstrations, which is what I'll be doing at the conference."

"All while wearing a Hawaiian lei around your neck," I quipped.

He flashed a full white grin. "Hey, when in Rome. What about you? What do you do? Whatever it is, it's gotta be more interesting than my job."

"I'm an interior designer. Still growing my business, but things are going *very* well these days."

"That's what's up. See, I told you I knew it would be more interesting than sales."

I giggled. "I guess you were."

"You ever been out to LA before?"

"This is my first time visiting Cali period. You?"

"I go back and forth to Silicon Valley a lot, so to me, Cali is like my second home. LA is dope, though. Are you gonna have time to squeeze in a little pleasure while you're out there?"

My shoulders rose and fell. "Not sure, but I hope so. I at least wanna grab some good food."

"If you're lookin' for somethin' quick, I'll say In-N-Out Burger. But if you're lookin' for somethin' more upscale, let's see; there's Nobu or Beauty & Essex."

"Thanks for the suggestions."

"No problem."

Our conversation spilled over into the next hour out of a six-hour flight. We chatted about our favorite east coast and west coast restaurants and how we thought the Hollywood Walk of Fame and Disneyland were both overrated tourist sites. Everything was perfect, and then *it* happened. He asked *the* question.

"I know I'll only have your attention for a few more hours before our paths split, but I've been enjoyin' our conversation," he told me.

I nodded. "Me too."

"I would love to get your number. Maybe we can connect in the air or on the ground again one of these days," he suggested. "That is if someone else doesn't have your attention."

"Are you asking me if I'm single?"

"Not to be too forward or anything, but yeah. Are you?"

"Um, it's complicated."

He bobbed his head. "I understand that. I've had one foot in and the other out of that boat a time or two myself."

I shook my head. "No. I don't even know why I said that. It's not complicated at all. I'm single," I confirmed.

I'd had a case of word vomit and decided to blame it on the champagne going to my head. Kas was over two-thousand miles away and was still silently lingering around like a shadow. Life had taken us down two separate paths, and I knew it was time to stop fighting the inevitable. He was married and having a baby, and I was focusing on my career. If anything, my conversation with Demari had proven one thing to me. As much as I wanted to leave Kas in my rearview, my heart wasn't ready to move on from him.

Thirteen

CANAAN

ONCE I'D BEEN VOTED in as the head of my family with all rights and privileges, Trinity and I tied the knot in a brief, private ceremony one weekend in Vegas. Soon after we said *I do*, Trinity decided she wanted to build a house instead of continuing to look for places around the city. She'd even started looking at land and new housing developments. She was trying her best to domesticate me, but she and I both knew I would always be a dog at heart.

As happy as she was, there was no way I could tell her it *wasn't* real. Yeah, we'd had our ceremony, but I never filed the marriage certificate to make it legal. There was no official record of our marriage in the court system, but I knew the symbolism of having my last name alone would pacify her. As far as I was concerned, what she didn't know wouldn't hurt her. Aside from that, I still hadn't come clean to her about Yara or her pregnancy. I'd pushed Yara to the cliff of my thoughts and shoved her ass right off. If she didn't want anything to do with me, then she could get the fuck on. I had more important shit to worry about.

I had to meet with Cena downtown to go over my father's estate, and I wasn't in the mood to be in the same room with her. I knew she would bring up the fact that I'd gone behind her back and taken our father's seat when she was away on her honeymoon. She'd even rushed back home early because of it. But I didn't care what she had to say. The moves had already been made, and the deal was done.

* * *

"MR. OLIVER WILL SEE YOU NOW," the receptionist announced.

I followed behind Cena and the receptionist into an office and sat down. Across from us sat Oliver Miller. He was a red-headed man with green eyes and a dark suit. He cleared his throat. "Cena, Canaan, nice to meet you."

"Hi," Cena responded while I gave him a silent head nod.

"As the appointed executor of your father's estate, it was my job to identify all of his assets and determine their value, then use them to pay off any debts or taxes. We're meeting today to discuss the distribution of his remaining assets. In addition to that, I will be providing you both copies of his will."

"Okay," Cena replied.

He jetted a hiss through a crack in his tight lips. "After careful assessment and the paying off his credit card debts and delinquent taxes, there is the matter of disbursement of the remainder of his fifteen-million-dollar life insurance policy."

My brows rose while I tried my best to contain a smile. "Fifteen *million*?"

"Yes."

"What about his investments, jewelry, and businesses?" Cena interjected.

"All those things were identified with his other assets, but your father's debts were substantial. I had to sell his shares to cover his back taxes and fees. I don't know how to say this gently, but your father's finances were in shambles."

"How much is left from the fifteen million?" I asked, cutting straight to the chase.

"And how much is left from our mother's life insurance policy?" Cena added.

Oliver sighed. "Nothing."

"What about the house and his cars?" I asked.

"It's paid off, and the property taxes are paid up. As for the vehicles, I'd advise you to liquidate them... the Rolls Royce, the Lexus, and the Range Rover."

"How much is left from the fifteen million?" I repeated after realizing I hadn't gotten a definite answer.

"One point two million dollars. Split between the two of you, that's six-hundred thousand dollars apiece."

"That's it? Out of fifteen fuckin' million dollars?" I quizzed, eyes narrowed on him.

"Again, your father's finances were in shambles. I would highly recommend an accountant to straighten this o—"

"How soon 'til we get the money?" I asked, cutting him off.

"I can have the checks cut this afternoon or the money wired into your respective accounts by the end of the day."

"Wire it," I told him before storming out of his office in a blaze of rage. I hadn't inherited shit but debt and headaches. Oliver had only paid off my father's legal obligations. Not one red cent had gone toward his gambling debts with the Rivera family. Seconds later, Cena came out.

"Did you know his debts were that bad? Of course, you did!" I accused.

"Shut up, Canaan! And lower your voice! I'm just as shocked as you are, okay?"

"You know he owes Ruiz Rivera."

"How much?"

"I don't know, but I know it's probably more than six hundred fuckin' thousand dollars."

"So, find out."

I scoffed. "And when I find out it's some crazy ass number and we have nothing to offer him, then what? Then what do we do? Huh?"

She folded her arms across her chest while shooting me a disapproving brow. "We? Don't you mean *you*?"

I sucked my teeth. "There it is. I knew you wouldn't stay silent for too long."

"You and I both know our father wanted me to be the head of our family, not you!"

"And yet, look at me. I'm on top! You can't fuckin' touch me, and it makes you sick!" I boasted.

"Why is everything always a fucking competition with you, huh? We're supposed to be family!"

"We might be family, but I don't like shit about you."

She scoffed. "What have I done for you not to like me, Canaan?"

"For one, I don't like how you always speakin' to me like I'm a child when I'm a grown-ass man!"

"You're a lot of things, Canaan, but a man, you are not. And it's not my job to make you one."

"See! There you go again! Talkin' down to me and shit! I run this shit, Cena! Get your ass in line and deal with it."

"I will fight you for this, and I *will* win," she warned me.

I stepped closer to her with my head cocked to the side. "Are you ready to go to war with your own family, Cena?"

"Are you?" she countered. "Is that why you killed our father?"

My brows creased. "Is that why I *what*?" I asked with a chuckle. "You sound desperate."

"Do I? I know you were there that night, and Lorraine didn't tell the police about it. Why is that, huh? Did you threaten her to keep quiet?" she accused.

I bit my lip. I'd paid Lorraine ten thousand dollars not to mention my name to the cops, but I didn't expect Cena to pick up on it. "I paid the bitch to keep my name out of it so that the police wouldn't be sniffin' around our fuckin' family business!" I reminded her.

Her eyes rolled skyward. "Yeah, okay."

"You think you can cast me out of my own family by pinning our father's death on me? I have an alibi, so I suggest you and your crazy ass allegations stay the fuck out of my way." I growled.

We stared each other down in a silent standoff before an incoming call interrupted. I peeled my eyes away from her long enough to look down at my phone and see that Julius was calling. I shifted away from her while placing the phone up to my ear.

"Hello? Yeah. I'm on my way," I told him before hanging up. I turned back to Cena, cutting my eyes at her one last time before stalking off.

* * *

FINDING out I had no money at my disposal to pay off my father's illegal gambling debts, right before I had to meet with his debtor, wasn't my idea of a good day. But Julius called, and I had no choice but to answer. When I arrived at his home, I saw a few other cars but thought nothing of it. Once inside, I pulled him to the side to discuss Cena and his game plan before meeting with Ruiz Rivera.

"Cena's asking questions. Well, not even questions, full-blown accusations about my father's death," I informed him.

"What kind of accusations?"

"That I had something to do with it. I told her ass she sounded desperate and that I had an alibi."

"Mmm. Do you think she's going to be a problem?"

I shook my head. "No. I can handle my sister," I confirmed.

I'd already gotten the upper hand on her once, and I knew if push came to shove, I could do the shit again.

He reached out to pat my shoulder. "Good. Is that all?"

"Yeah."

"Okay. Let's go."

"Hold up. I know you set up this meeting for us to meet with Ruiz, but what's your game plan here?" I asked Julius.

The doorbell chimed before he could answer. Instead of pushing out a response, he huffed out a long breath and swaggered toward the door. I stood at the end of the hall, watching as Ruiz Rivera and a few of his men walked in, followed by Douglass Simms and his men. My eyes doubled in size. What the fuck was this? An ambush? I cleared my throat while making my way toward the group of men in the foyer.

"Now that we're all here, let's go to my meeting room," Julius announced.

We all followed him inside his dimly lit meeting space and sat around a long table that seated ten. He took his seat at the head, and I, to his right. As much as I knew better than to have an outburst, I couldn't hold my tongue. "What the fuck are they doin' here?" I asked with a grimace across my face. I narrowed my eyes at Douglass Simms and jabbed my finger in his direction.

"We were invited just like you, nigga," his second-in-command barked.

I pushed myself away from the table, ready to throw hands, while Julius, Ruiz, and Douglass remained seated. The real reason he'd brought us all together still hadn't become clear to me, but there wasn't shit I needed to discuss in the presence of my enemies.

Julius held out his hands before speaking calmly. "Gentlemen, take your seats. And I'm not asking."

We kept our eyes trained on each other, snarling and snapping like two hungry dogs.

"Yo, for real, what the fuck are my family's enemies doing sitting at the same table as me? This shit goes against everything in The Order! I'm not sitting down with these niggas until somebody tells me what is goin' on!" I refused.

"We are here to discuss your father's shady business deals, Canaan, which involves my land, which was the same land promised to Ruiz to build his casinos on."

"I still don't understand why we need to talk about that in front of them," I stated.

"Douglass Simms is here because of me," Julius announced.

"The territory my father sold you, what happens to it now? Who will deal in it? Us... or them?"

"The Simms family will be dealing on that territory, and in return, I get a lucrative cut each month."

I glanced across the table. A teasing smile crossed Douglass number two's face. "Better get down on them ashy ass knees and pledge your loyalty, nigga. It's our time now!" he boasted.

My brow creased. It took everything for me not to jump across the table and beat his face in. Instead, I turned my attention back to Julius, immediately realizing why my father said he didn't trust him. "That gives you a monopoly on the state! That's exactly why my father didn't want to sell you his territory!"

"Unfortunately for him, he couldn't shake his gambling demons, and in exchange for my help paying off his debts, he signed that land over to me. So unless you're prepared to pay me back for all the loans I gave him in addition to what he owes Ruiz, I can do whatever the fuck I want," he confirmed.

"How much does he owe in total?"

Julius and Ruiz looked at each other before looking back at me. "Two point five million," Ruiz answered.

My heart sunk to the soles of my feet, and my thoughts returned to the meeting I'd had earlier. The six hundred thousand wasn't even a drop in the bucket. Julius Barnes and every other family head were concerned with money, power, and respect. The Order's foundation was based on loyalty and family, but I felt like I'd gotten into bed with a bunch of snakes.

"So, where does this leave me?"

Ruiz cleared my throat. "As the new head of your family, I expect you to honor your father's deal. I will still build my casinos on your territory, just in a different section. Instead of you getting a cut, I will keep it *all* until your father's debt is settled."

Julius added, "Make no mistake, young blood, this *is* the new plan. You can either agree or..." He let his sentence trail off, forcing me to fill in the blank.

The table fell silent before I dipped my chin in a reluctant nod. My hands were fuckin' tied. If I didn't fall in line, I knew Julius and Ruiz would do anything to cut my family and me out of The Order. My father's operation was in the red. I needed to push out twice as much product to ensure I could continue putting food on the table.

"I need to hear you fuckin' say it," Julius demanded.

I bit my lip before nodding. "Yeah. Aight. Okay."

My head was spinning. In a matter of minutes, I'd gone from sitting on top of the world to being crushed under the weight of it. I couldn't believe Julius had helped me get what I wanted only to sell me out to my enemies. I didn't know whether to be more pissed off at myself for trusting him in the first place or my father for making messy ass business deals before he died and leaving me to clean up his mess. Either way, I was fucked. Shit hit differently when you were no longer at the top.

KAS

"*I GOT* *Lori Harvey on my wish list.*" I rapped alongside Meek Mill's "Going Bad" inside the shower before my music cut off mid-verse. A second later, my phone began to ring.

"Yeah." I answered for Cena while continuing to wash my body.

"You home? We need to talk."

"I'm here. Come through."

"I'm on my way," she informed me before ending the call.

Twenty minutes later, the elevators to my penthouse opened, and Cena stepped inside with a frazzled look on her face. I could tell by the sound of her voice over the phone that shit had gone left, so I had a bottle of liquor sitting on the counter for myself and a bottle of ice water for her since I knew she couldn't drink.

"How'd the meeting go?" I asked her. She cut her eyes at me as if to ask *how you think it went?* "That bad, huh?" I followed up.

She scoffed as her heels clicked across my floor. "Yeah. It was *that* bad."

"Exactly how bad are we talkin'?"

"Let's just say I wish I could be the one with the liquor instead of this water," she said before swiping the bottle off the counter.

"Tell me what happened," I insisted before taking a sip of my drink.

Frustration sat lightly on her face. "Canaan was the asshole he always is. He blew up and stormed out once he found out my father—" She paused.

"Your father what?"

She released a drawn-out exhale. "His debts are more... substantial than we thought. He had a fifteen-million-dollar insurance policy, and after paying off all of his debts and back taxes, there was a little over a million left to split between my brother and me."

"So, what's the problem? At least y'all get a little somethin'."

"The problem is, only my father's legal debts were paid. This has nothing to do with anything he owes to the families in The Order for his gambling. My father was bad with money."

"So what are you going to do?"

She scoffed. "You mean besides watch Canaan drown? At this point, I'm starting to think he did me a favor."

"You still plan to fight him for it?"

"I do, but I'm waiting to see how this all plays out right now. When we first got back here, I felt rushed, like I needed all the chips to fall together right away, but now I'm playing for the long term," she assured me.

I nodded. "Okay."

"In other news, I accused him of killing our father," she announced while huffing out a humored breath.

My eyebrows jogged up my forehead. "What did he say?"

"Um, let's see. He told me I was delusional. Oh, and he said he had an alibi."

"What was it?"

"He didn't say."

"I remember I saw him leaving my father's house after I left you at the hospital."

"Yeah, I know."

"I mean, I'll follow your lead with all this when it comes to your brother, but I am curious to know why it seems like my father is helping Canaan so much."

"Are you going to ask him?" she quizzed.

"Hell yeah," I told her while grabbing my phone.

The phone rang a few times before he picked up. "Yes, Kasim," he answered.

"Hey. You busy?"

"Going over some shipment information at home in my study," he informed me. "Why?"

"Bet. I'm about to pull up on you. There's somethin' I want to talk to you about face to face."

* * *

THE FLOOR CREAKED underneath my feet as I shuffled inside my father's study twenty minutes later. He peered up at me from behind his desk. "You wanted to see me?" he asked.

"Yeah."

"How was your honeymoon?"

I hadn't spoken to my father outside of business since the wedding. I'd been holding off on confronting him about why he'd chosen to help Canaan behind my back.

"Short," I responded, "but you already knew that."

His features drew tight. "I'm proud of you, son."

"For what? Being your fall guy or your back-up plan? Because I can't tell."

His brow raised in confusion. "You got somethin' you need to get off your chest? Or was it your intention to come over here and gripe at me?"

I stepped closer to him. "I came here because I wanna know why you're protecting Canaan and worked with him to take over for his family when I told you his father wanted Cena to do it."

Hesitation pinwheeled across his face before he spoke. "Close the door." I trekked backward to shut the door, and he spoke again. "What makes you think I'm protecting him?"

My right brow crept toward my hairline. "Aren't you?"

"He's served his purpose to me," he disclosed.

"What does that mean?"

"He met with Ruiz, Douglass, and me. There's a new plan, and Canaan has agreed to follow it."

"What new plan?"

"I told him Douglass will deal on my territory, and Ruiz will build his new casinos on another part of the McQueen's territory."

"And he was okay with that?"

"What other choice did he have? He wanted to sit in the big chair, so he had to be ready to take on the big chair responsibilities. We all know he won't be able to sustain his lifestyle with little to no territory to sell on. He's going to have to work twice as hard. And we both know it's only a matter of time before the McQueens are dissolved completely."

"I don't understand why you looked out for him only to tear him down."

"Silas is gone, and Canaan was always expendable. Besides, he's not... never mind."

"What? Say it," I demanded.

"What I'm about to tell you can't leave this room."

"What is it? Is it about Canaan?"

"It's about Silas and his children, including your wife."

"What about them?"

A pensive sigh escaped past his lips. "Silas wanted a son *so* bad. The minute he found out his wife was pregnant, that's all he ever talked about. Your mother and I had already had Koda, so I knew first-hand the joy of having a son, and I wanted that for him. His wife insisted on them not knowing the sex until she delivered. And when she did, she delivered two healthy, bouncing baby *girls*. A set of fraternal twins who were born three minutes apart."

A look of shock passed over my features. "Hold up. Two *girls*?"

"Yes. That's what I said," he confirmed.

"So you're telling me that Cena and Canaan aren't twins?"

"No. They're not related by blood at all."

I stood across from my father, frozen in shock. Silas's secrets had come pouring out like rain from beyond the grave, leaving no stone unturned. I knew the news would crush Cena if she ever found out, but maybe a part of her would be relieved to know she wasn't related to Canaan's unpredictable ass.

Confusion tangled my brow as I struggled to find my words. "W-what the fuck, Pa? What the fuck did he do? What happened to his other daughter? And who the fuck is Canaan?"

He shook his head. "An out-of-state adoption was supposed to be arranged. I didn't have anything to do with it after the... switch."

"Whose son is Canaan if he isn't Silas's?"

"He was a low-life dealer with debts to me. The boy was his fourth kid. He was born the same day as Silas's girls. He could barely afford to feed the ones he had. In my eyes, we did him and Canaan a favor."

"You paid a man for his son?"

"Silas paid him."

"How much?"

"Fifty thousand," he replied.

"And what did you get out of the deal?"

"What do you mean?"

I shifted my weight from one leg to the other. "You taught me a long time ago, nothing in this business is for free."

"Silas paid him fifty thousand dollars for the baby, and since he owed me, I took half of that."

My eyebrows leaped up, and my face opened wide with shock. "You made twenty-five thousand off a newborn baby's head? You're ruthless. That's sick."

"That's business," he corrected me.

"Who else knows?"

"No one but us."

It had always been instilled in us to make alliances and relationships with people who ran in the same wealthy circles as us, but I never thought for one second that Cena and Canaan weren't blood. My mind jumped to one conclusion after another, finally landing on Jrue's ancestry DNA test. I knew she shared the same birthday as Cena and Canaan, but I was curious to learn more.

"What hospital?"

"Kasim, why does this matter? It was a long time ago. Soon, the McQueen family will be out of The Order, and you'll be able to dissolve your marriage to Cena."

"Because it does! It all matters! Tell me what hospital they were born at!"

"Cranberry Hill Memorial Hospital," he answered.

"I have to go," I announced, pacing toward the door.

"Don't go off and do something you'll regret," he warned to my back before the door slammed behind me.

As soon as I slammed my body inside the driver's seat, I tapped away at my phone screen to call Kamil. The engine revved, and his voice came through my car speakers. "What up, bul?" he answered.

"Mil, I need you to find someone to look into some birth records for me."

"Birth records? For what? What's going on?" he asked.

"No questions, aight? Can you do it or not?"

"Okay, chill. I got you. Just tell me what you need exactly."

"All the birth, death, and adoption records of anyone born at Cranberry Hill Memorial Hospital on October 31, 1998," I briefed him. "Let me know what they find ASAP."

Fifteen

JRUE

I PUSHED through the bank's thick glass doors and sailed back onto the bustling sidewalk filled with shoppers, dog walkers, and blue-collar workers. They all had someplace different to be for various reasons, while I'd just cashed my final payment from a local design job. The meeting in L.A. went amazing, and I was all set to head home and pack my bags for the design job of a lifetime on the West Coast that would be starting in a few days. I was excited to put some distance between the City of Brotherly Love and me for a few weeks and even more excited to see my business bank account triple in size.

As things would have it, I was currently all smiles and thriving. My teeth-exposed grin instantly vanished when I spotted Kas at a latte stand across the street. I froze mid-step, bumping shoulders with a jogger passing by. It was as if the nigga had a sixth sense because the minute I laid eyes on him, he looked past the city buses and honking cars passing by and straight at me.

His face lit up. "Jrue!"

"Shit," I murmured before spotting my car parked along the curb. "Shit, shit, shit."

I hurried to it before he called out my name again. "Jrue!"

The night I kicked him out of my apartment, I made the

conscious decision to block him again. I didn't need any more late-night backslides. I tried to keep walking amid Kas repetitively calling out my name. As far as I was concerned, there was nothing left to say.

I snapped my neck in his direction, staring aimlessly as he darted across multi-lane traffic to get to me. He made his way through the sea of pedestrians on the sidewalk until we were standing face to face. He had the freshest haircut and was draped in a crisp white tee, a navy blazer, and khaki joggers.

"Jrue," he said, slightly winded from his run, "hey."

"Hey... That was some impressive running you did there."

His brown eyes sparkled with laughter. "And I didn't spill a drop of my coffee," he boasted.

I darted my eyes away from him, focusing my attention on the pile of cigarette butts gathered in the gutter, then to the narrow alleyway to my left—anything to keep my knees from liquefying.

"Jrue," he said, calling my attention back to him. He looked at me, gaze soft as silk. "You look... beautiful."

I cleared my throat to swallow a smile. "Thanks."

"How have you been?"

"Good," I replied, keeping my conversation as short as possible.

"You, uh, just came from the bank?" he quizzed before sipping his coffee.

I could tell he was doing his best to make conversation, no matter how dry I was trying to be. "Yeah. Wrapping up some final business here before I leave," I announced.

A spark of confusion ignited in his eyes. "Leave? Where to?"

"L.A., I'll be, uh, doing some work for a celebrity client."

I watched the muscle beside his eye twitch. "Is it permanent?"

"It's only for a few weeks, but who knows? My business is starting to take me places, and I'm just along for the ride."

He bobbed his head. "Wow, uh. Congratulations."

Although he'd just congratulated me, there was a mournful look in his eyes. I cleared my throat. "I guess congratulations are in order for you, too," I blurted out.

"What are you talking about?"

I side-eyed him while cocking my head to the side. "Are we still pretending I don't know?"

"Is this about the wedding? I already told you that's just—"

Frustration stirred behind my eyes. "I know about your baby, Kas," I cut him off. "I know Cena is pregnant; excuse me, your wife."

"Hold up. You have the wrong idea, Jrue. It's not mine."

My brows shot up, surprised that he was still able to lie to my face so effortlessly. "Wow. You still can't drop the act, huh? There's no reason to hide behind all that bullshit you fed me about your family obligations and business ties anymore, Kas. I know the truth!"

"You don't know shit!" The frost in his gaze said more to me than his words. "Just stop and listen to what I have to tell you, aight? I don't wanna hear shit come out your mouth until I'm fuckin' finished! You hear me, Jrue?" he challenged, not caring that we were hashing out our emotions in public.

I sucked my teeth. "Can we at least get in the car and finish this conversation? People are starting to fucking stare," I announced.

"Fine."

I unlocked the doors, and we both fell inside. Once the doors were closed, I turned my attention to him. "Say what you gotta say."

A long breath seeped from his lungs. "The baby isn't mine. She has someone else. She's always had someone else."

"Hold up, what?"

"I didn't find out about her pregnancy until the day of our wedding. I tried to leave."

I nodded. "Yara told me."

"Hold up. Is that how you found out about the baby?"

"Yeah."

"Listen, I know this shit keeps getting messier, but you have to believe a nigga, Jrue. I wouldn't lie to you. Not about this. Not anymore. We are only tied together for business reasons, like I told you."

My gaze went remote for a few seconds while I tried to process everything he said. My pride was a tough pill to swallow, but I was willing to admit I was wrong for skydiving off a cliff of conclusions without asking him. But in my defense, it *did* come from a reliable source.

A sigh slumped me against the driver's seat. "I'm sorry. I should've talked to you first. I guess I was just scared of what the answer would be if I did ask."

"I meant what I said, Jrue. You're still the only one I want," he assured me.

"I hear you, but I don't know."

"What don't you know?"

"I don't know if I can trust you, and at the end of the day, you're *still* married, even if it is for the reasons you say they are."

"I miss the shit out of you," he publicized to only the two of us, showing no regard for my last comment.

I sighed. "Kas..."

He pivoted his body in my direction. "Can I ask you something personal?"

"That depends on what it is," I said with a lazy shrug.

"What hospital were you born at?"

My eyes tightened at the corners. "What? Why?"

"I wanna know."

"Okay, but why do you want to know something like that?"

"I told you it was personal."

"Are you looking into me? Better yet, is your family looking into me?" I asked, eyes slanted at him.

He tossed up the palms of his hands to calm me. "No. It's nothing like that. Trust me."

I scoffed before mumbling, "There we go with *that* word again. Tell me why you want to know."

"Tell me the hospital first, and then I'll tell you."

I levied a silent glare at him before huffing out a short breath. "Cranberry Hill Memorial Hospital."

"And your birthday? You said your birthday was on Halloween, right?"

My chin dipped in a reluctant nod. "Yeah. Why?"

"Did you ever decide to do that blood test with your sister?" he asked.

Surprise brightened the whites of my eyes. "What the hell is going on, Kas? Why are you asking me about my birthday and now about my sister? What is going on? Tell me!" I demanded.

"Please, Jrue. Just answer my questions, and I promise it will all make sense, or maybe it won't, but please. Tell me, aight?"

My lungs flattened. "We did a DNA swab."

"And?" he asked eagerly.

"It was zero percent, okay? I'm fuckin' adopted! But even still, I don't know what that has to do with why you're asking me all of this personal shit out of the blue!"

"It has everything to do with you," he confirmed.

I sigh-growled. "What has everything to do with me, Kas? I'm fuckin' lost here."

Kas blew air out of his cheeks. "On October 31, 1998, a boy and a set of twin girls were all born within minutes of each other at Cranberry Hill Memorial Hospital."

"Okay, and?"

"You said you were adopted, right?"

"Yeah. So?" I asked, snapping my eyes at him.

"A set of twin girls were born, but a boy and a girl went home together, while the other twin girl was adopted. I think *you* were the other twin, Jrue."

I shot him a round-eyed expression. "What the fuck are you saying to me right now, Kas? And how do you even know all of this?"

"I'm saying... I think you're my wife's twin sister."

* * *

INSTEAD OF GOING HOME to pack for L.A. like I had planned, I headed straight to my mother's house, dying to get clarity, anything to keep my head from spinning away from my body. I caught her coming out of the house the minute I swung my car into her driveway. I made sure to block her car so she couldn't escape me. After throwing the gear shift into park, I hopped out of the car to run up to her.

"Tell me it's not true."

Her brow creased in confusion. "Tell you what's not true, Jrue?" she asked while giving me a once-over. "What's wrong? You're shaking."

"Don't worry about that. I need to talk to you about something important."

"Can it wait? I've got to get to the hospital. My shift starts in an hour, and you know how traffic can be this time of day."

I shook my head incessantly. "No. It can't wait."

"Okay, then spill it. What's on your mind? Or what do you need to get off your chest?"

"Is Charity home?" I asked with a sigh.

"No. Not yet. Why?"

"I told her not to say anything to you, but the two of us did an ancestry DNA test some weeks ago."

"And?"

"And things came back weird. I didn't match up with you, her, or dad's results."

"Where did you get our results?"

"I had Charity find them in your closet where you keep all the important documents."

"You two were snooping through my things when I'm not around?" Her voice escalated, but I wasn't about to let her change the subject.

"Focus, Mama. That's not the point of this conversation, and you know it. We did a DNA swab. I know Charity and I aren't blood sisters... that I'm not related to any of you."

Her eyes continued downward to the Skechers on her feet before I saw a tear drop from her face and hit the pavement. Her silence, coupled with her body language, said it all. "So, it's true then? It's not a figment of my imagination anymore. It's real. I-I'm adopted," I prompted her.

"Let's go inside," she insisted.

"No," I refused. "Tell me right here, right now."

"Cut your car off and come inside the house, Jrue. I'll tell you everything once you do," she said before walking back inside.

Irritation blasted from my lungs before I turned on my heels to kill the engine and follow in her footsteps. "So?" I asked from the doorframe.

"Close the door and sit down," she instructed.

"I'm fine right here," I stated, arms folded tightly across my chest.

She thrust out a breath. "You always were stubborn. Ever since the day I brought you home from the hospital."

"I want to know everything."

"This is hard for me, okay? I never thought..."

"What? That you'd have to come clean to me about the truth? How could you lie to me all these years about something this big, Mama? This is my life!" I argued, eyes misting over.

"Don't you think I know that? And that's exactly what prevented me from saying anything to you for all these years."

"Twenty-five years!" I reminded her. "You chose to lie to me for twenty-five years, for what? To spare your own feelings?"

"I wanted to tell you, but your father kept pushing it off. We wanted to tell you on your sixteenth birthday. Then you remember what happened?"

"Yeah. I broke my arm the night of my party."

"Right. So, then we said, okay, we'll try again at eighteen. That way, if you wanted to know more, you'd be legally able to go out and find out whatever."

"And then Dad had his first heart attack," I chimed in.

"Yup. So then it became something we just kept kicking down the road. Another milestone would come, and something else would happen, and it just... it never felt like the right time."

"Did you know my birth parents?" I asked.

She quickly shook her head as moisture began to collect on her lids. "No. I knew nothing about them. I'd only been working as a pediatric nurse in that hospital for a few months. The man that handed you off to me said that he wanted it to be an out-of-state adoption and that they wanted no rights to the baby."

Silent tears tracked one another down my cheeks. "So, they willingly threw me away like I was nothing?"

"You weren't nothing, Jrue. You were far from nothing. Your father and I tried for years to get pregnant. *Years.* And it just... Anyway, I saw you, and I don't know. Everything in me just melted. Fresh out the womb, and I could tell you were such a bright light," she boasted as tears gummed up her throat.

I licked the salty tears from my lips. "And so, you decided to adopt me? Just like that?"

"And I'd do it again," she assured me. "You've always been mine, since the moment I saw you. The way you gripped my finger so tight. I knew you were a fighter. I knew you were mine. So yeah, you were supposed to be adopted by an out-of-state family, but I stepped in."

"And what about Charity, Mama? How is she supposed to feel about all of this? I remember seeing you pregnant with her, so I know she's your daughter."

She dipped her chin. "Yes. Like I said, we tried for so long to have a baby. You were eight when I got pregnant with Charity. It was unexpected because I thought I'd closed that chapter in my life. She was our miracle child, but so were you. I don't want you to lose sight of that."

"I don't know what to say."

She pushed out a heavy exhale. "I'm sorry you had to find out the way you did. I should've told you. I'm hoping we can... heal from this."

She reached out to embrace me, and I took a step back. "I'm sorry, Mama, but I... I just need some time to process all of this. I hope you can understand that."

A sigh shuttled through her lips while she nodded. "I do. We can talk more when you're ready. *If* you're ready."

I turned to leave almost as quickly as I came, unable to stomach the truth. My birth parents took one look at me and decided to discard me like trash with no explanation why. A part of me felt like I should've been grateful. Had I been brought up by my birth parents, who knows what kind of privileged yet limited life I would've had? I was not interested in discovering who they were or anything else about them. If they didn't want shit to do with me, I would be sure to keep that same energy.

Finding out the news only made me want to get the hell out of Philly faster. I fought back the tears the entire drive home as I headed there to pack my bags. The floodgates opened the second I sailed through the front door. My mascara-spiked eyes misted with tears as my ribs fell into a turbulent exhale. For the first time in my life, I was broken and confused about who I thought I was.

"Jrue?" Yara called out.

I looked up at her with watery vision. "H-hey."

"What happened? What's wrong?"

I recovered my breath while choking back a sob. "It's nothing. I'm okay."

"Bullshit. You're falling apart in the middle of our apartment as we speak," she reminded me as if I wasn't already aware.

I shook my head. "I don't want to talk about it right now. I-I just can't."

Yara hurried over to me and pulled me into a lung-compressing clutch, and I sobbed even harder. Without asking any questions or uttering another word, she began to rub my back and make shushing noises to calm me. "Whatever it is, I'm here."

I slowly nodded before breaking away from her embrace. "I'm going to go wash the day off," I informed her.

"Okay. I'm only a hallway away if you need me."

"Thanks."

I climbed into bed thirty minutes later, and my mind still felt like it was swirling the drain. My head hit the pillow, and my lids came down with ease. Sleeping would be easy. I knew it would be waking up and feeling the cyclic ache in my chest again that would tear me apart.

Sixteen

KAS

Four and a half weeks later

MY CAR WAS PARKED curbside at airport arrivals with the blinkers on while I leaned against the passenger side door cradling a bouquet of two dozen red roses in my arm. It had been weeks since I dropped the bomb on Jrue about her potentially being my wife's sister. She'd been off in Los Angeles, doing her thing, but I was happy she agreed to let me pick her up from the airport. The automatic terminal doors whooshed open and closed as a sea of people disbursed through them every few minutes. My eyes searched for a familiar face in the crowd until they landed on Jrue.

I instantly found myself unable to look away, unable to do anything but study her. I noted how her wild, bark-brown and black curls were blowing in the slight breeze or how her colorful bicycle shorts, oversized T-shirt, and platform Converse all complemented each other. She looked more beautiful than I remembered.

"Jrue," I called out while waving her down with my free arm.

Her glinting eyes landed on mine before she dropped her gaze down to the flowers. "Are these for me?" she asked when she approached me.

"Of course."

Jrue hesitated before reaching out to take them and burying her face in them. She inhaled deeply and smiled. "Mmm. They smell nice."

"I wish they actually smelled as good as you make them look like they do."

"What do you mean? They smell delicious," she replied before opening the passenger door and getting inside.

"I'm glad you like them."

She nodded while cradling the delicate stems like a newborn baby. "It was a pleasant surprise after a long six-hour flight. Thanks."

"Let me take your bags," I insisted before fishing my keys out of my pocket and popping my trunk.

I closed her door before putting her bags in the back and getting in on my side. My index finger jammed the push-to-start button while I twisted my neck in her direction. In a closed-in space, I could smell the scent of clean cotton and the ocean radiating off her walnut-brown skin. She smelled like sun-drenched linen at a beach house.

"How was L.A.? You look relaxed. Skin all sun kissed and shit like a Cali girl," I joked.

She smacked her teeth. "You know I'ma always be a Philly girl at heart, but the West Coast owes me nothing," she assured me with a bright smile. "Even though it was work, I still needed the space."

"Congrats on all of your business ventures, for real. I'm proud of you. I mean that shit."

Another smile stretched across her face. "Thanks. That means a lot coming from you."

"Why me?"

"Because you're the one who opened the door for me with the clientele I was trying to reach. You know that."

I nodded. As much as I didn't want to kill the upbeat vibe of our surface-level conversation, I knew there were important things we had to discuss. I cleared my throat while darting my eyes up to my rearview mirror and then my right-side mirror before switching lanes. "Are you ready for this?"

Jrue wagged her head from left to right, shaking her loose curls across her face. "No. Absolutely not. I still can't believe you got me to agree to this."

"You had over a month to change your mind," I reminded her.

"And I did! Like three times! You remember?"

"Ain't no takin' it back now. I've already kept Cena on ice too long about all of this, and she's ready to get some answers. We're getting to the bottom of this today."

"I still think this is the craziest shit ever." She scoffed. "It's insane, is what it is. I mean, I go my whole life, a whole twenty-five fucking years, thinking I know everything about myself, who I am, and where I come from, and then, bam! Now I might have a whole other family I knew nothing about and a twin fuckin' sister? A twin? A whole twin!" she exclaimed before she hid her face behind her hands.

After I dropped the bomb on Jrue that she might have been Cena's twin sister, I spent damn near every day digging further into their background to get some answers while she was gone. Following a round of the silent treatment, making up her mind, changing it, and then changing it back again, Jrue begrudgingly agreed to a private sit down with Cena, so the three of us could get everyone's truth out on the table. I pulled into my private entrance and heard Jrue release a pensive breath when I shut the car off.

"What's wrong?" I asked while turning to look at her.

"I don't think I—"

"Don't think, Jrue," I advised, cutting her off. "Don't think about shit. We are about to go in here and talk. That's it. You don't have to do anything more than that."

Her lungs flattened. "I know that. I just don't know if I'm ready to find out some shit I would've been better off not knowing in the first place, you know?"

"I do."

"All of this is new for me, emotionally. I had a lot of time to think when I wasn't working in L.A., and this shit really did a number on me..."

"I can see the worry in your eyes. What's the most overwhelming emotion you feel right now?"

Her eyes downturned before she shrugged her lean shoulders. "I don't know. I don't feel in control of anything right now. Like, I'm dealing with an emptiness I never knew I had and all these unwarranted feelings of abandonment and mistrust. A part of me feels like I'll never be good enough for two people I didn't even know existed three months ago. And I feel crazy saying that because I don't feel like I missed out on anything growing up. I know for a fact that my parents loved me. The people who raised me loved me. But, even knowing that, it still doesn't erase the feelings of unworthiness. Like, y'all took one look at me at birth, as a *baby*, and said, yeah, no. We don't want her. Like, that's hard for me," she confessed, choking back tears.

Jrue's coffee-brown eyes glimmered with unshed tears, and it was like seeing her clearly for the first time. She was like freshly fallen snow, beautiful but frigid. A mess of beautiful chaos with untamed curls, determination, and crazy dope creativity. It didn't matter if she was nobody to everyone else. She was everything to me.

"You have every right to feel that way, but you do know that you're amazing, right? You don't need to blame yourself or feel less than because you're out here being your own boss, making your own moves, and doing the shit on your terms. Everybody can't say that, especially not me and Cena," I reminded her.

She shot her swimming gaze to me as moisture spilled over the rim. "Thanks."

I reached across to hug her, pulling her as tight to my chest as I could. "I mean that shit. I know you're anxious, aight? I'm just hoping today brings you a little peace."

"I think having you here, watching me go through this in real-time is making me more frazzled," she confessed while pulling away.

"For real?"

"Yeah."

"I know I might not be able to help you too much through this, but I'm here to talk whenever. You already know I care about you. I don't want you to go through this alone."

"I appreciate you, Kas. I do."

"You know I'm here for you, right? Like, you can call me whenever, wherever, and I got you."

She nodded. "I do."

I smirked. "Tell me you trust a nigga."

"You know that's hard for me," she replied before smacking her lips.

"You don't have to shy away from me, Jrue."

"Growing up, my dad taught my sister and me that showing your emotions to people is like bleeding right next to a shark, and you should know by now that I'm the poster child for trust issues. I mean, if my own parents can lie to me, who can I trust?"

"Damn."

"I *do* want to trust you, Kas... just don't push me to do it, aight?"

"Bet. You're right." I agreed before swinging open the driver's side door.

"But the hug did help," she added when she stepped out of the car.

I changed directions and wheeled around to give her the kind of hug I wanted to in the first place. My arms encircled her waist, and I pulled her to my chest. "I'll give you as many hugs as you need," I assured her. "You feel good as hell in my arms."

I didn't know about her, but I felt the sparks when her skin brushed against mine. I wanted to hug her until she smelled like me.

After a few silent minutes of her head against my chest, she broke away and said, "Aight, I'm ready now. Let's do this."

The entire elevator ride up to my place, I tried my best not to kiss her senselessly and tell her I couldn't get her out of my head. It was the first time we'd been alone together at my home in a long time, and all I wanted were her lips against mine.

"Why are you staring at me?" she asked.

"Does it make you nervous when I stare?"

"No. Not nervous. A little annoyed, maybe. Or a little flattered, I guess," Jrue replied, the corners of her eyes crinkling as she grinned.

I looked down at my phone to see a text from Cena, saying she was on her way, just as the metal doors opened.

"She'll be here soon," I informed Jrue.

She stepped out, looking around as she inched deeper inside. "I guess this feels like a safe space."

My brow creased to a frown. "What you mean, you guess? You're with me. I'm your safe space," I solidified.

She cut her eyes at me before softening them to a playful look. "You can't say things like that to me."

"Why not when it's the truth?"

Her lashes beat softly. "You're married, remember?"

"Yeah, I'm married, but I'm not lettin' you break up with me again."

A laugh burst through her lips. "Oh my God. Did you *not* just hear that sentence out loud? And I feel like I've said this before, but I didn't know we were together to officially break up the first time."

"I want us to start over," I announced.

"And I want a healthy relationship, one where we don't have to lie or keep secrets from each other."

"We can have that."

She shook her head. "No, we can't. I want a soul connection, not just some *basic* relationship. I want to be in a relationship where we grow closer, not one that ruins trust," she explained.

"Like I said, we can have that. We can be all that. I want you and only you."

"I don't even know why we're talking about this because you still have a *wife*..."

I cut her off. "Let's meet again for the first time. I'll never be the version of me that lied to you and kept shit from you again. Tell me you can picture us together, Jrue, because I can."

"I can't talk about what I came here to talk about and us too. I just can't," she said while wagging her head from side to side.

"I can respect that. Just know that I think everything about you is beautiful, and you ain't gotta hide your scars from me."

"And what about your scars?"

I shrugged while making my way into the kitchen. "What about them?"

"Are you hiding yours from me?"

"I'm trying not to. I'm tellin' you, Jrue, a nigga tryna be all in with you."

"What does that even look like? You know what? Don't answer that. At least not right now. Let me just get through the rest of the day."

I tipped my chin in a nod. "Well, can I get you anything? At least fix you a drink? Maybe another hug?" I offered.

She tilted her head to the side before swiping some hair behind her ears. "You and these hugs."

"Is that a yes?"

She shrugged. "It's not a no."

I smiled before closing the gap between us and gathering her in my arms. We were two damaged souls, trying to heal from our pasts and lick our wounds. It wasn't perfect, but it felt like home. It felt like our own version of love.

"What if I kissed you right now?" I quizzed.

She looked up at me. "Kas—"

"Would you stop me?"

"Now is not the time for—"

I held her tighter. "Would you?"

She tried to pull her arms out from underneath mine, but I kept my chest crushed against hers. "Kas," she said, demanding my attention.

I leaned in to steal a quick kiss. When she didn't immediately push away from my grasp, I kissed her again—this time, slow enough to savor the sweet, stolen moment on borrowed time.

My cell chimed. "Cena's coming up," I announced without bothering to look at my phone.

I kissed her forehead lightly before she pulled away from me. A few seconds later, Cena arrived with her jaw-length bob swinging as she sailed inside. She stopped a few feet away from Jrue.

"Jrue, right?" she asked her.

"Yeah. And you're Cena?"

"Yes. Thank you for agreeing to meet with me, well... us," she said, tearing her eyes over to me. "Hey, Kasim."

"What's up?"

"I'm not going to lie. It took a lot for him to get me to come here. I know the first time we met was a bit... odd," Jrue admitted to her.

"Yeah, but I'm sure Kasim has explained our arrangement to you. I promise you; I don't see him as anything more than a trusted friend. Our marriage is on paper only."

"And the baby," I started to add before she cut me off.

"Is definitely not his."

"So you have someone else?"

Cena nodded. "His name is Liam, and no, my family doesn't know about him."

"Wow. You two actually did just get married for your families," she realized.

"That's what I've been trying to tell you," I told Jrue.

"It hits different hearing it from her," she told me before turning her attention back to Cena. "Should we... you know, sit down?" Jrue offered.

"Yeah, let's do it."

The three of us entered my living room and sat on opposite couches. Having the two of them in the same room was a little trippy for me, especially knowing I'd fallen for one and was legally married to the other. Cena was a few shades lighter than Jrue, but they both had warm brown eyes, full lips, and petite frames.

"I guess I should start with what brought you two together in the first place," I started.

Cena held out her hand to stop me. "I think I wanna hear from Jrue first, if you don't mind. Like, how did all of this come to be for you? Because I don't know about you, but I'm still shocked. Kasim has been leaving me on ice, not wanting to explain all the details until we were together."

Jrue sighed. "Yeah, um, my life has been... a rollercoaster, to say the least. It all started a couple of months ago when my little sister, Charity, wanted me to get this stupid ancestry DNA kit for her. I got it, we both turned it in, and when I got the results, nothing matched up with anyone in my family. That was when things first got weird."

"And then what happened?"

"After a lot of research and back and forth, we decided to go ahead and put all the suspicions to rest and do the DNA swab. No match."

"So it was then that you knew you were adopted?"

"I didn't want to believe it, but it hit differently when I saw that zero percent match with the DNA test."

"What all do you know about my... *our* parents?" Cena asked her.

Jrue shook her head. "Nothing. I talked to my mother after Kas told me that we could possibly be sisters, and she confirmed that I was adopted."

"What all did she say?"

"She said she didn't know my birth parents and that she'd only been working as a pediatric nurse in the hospital where I was born for a few months. She told me that a man handed me off to her and said that he wanted it to be an out-of-state adoption and that the parents wanted no rights to me."

"Did she describe his appearance or get his name?" I asked her.

"No. None of that."

"And that's all you know?"

"Yeah," Jrue answered.

"And Kas, how did you get involved in all of this?" Cena asked, turning her attention to me.

"I went to my father to ask about his relationship with Canaan and why it seemed like he was always in his corner. Then he started spilling one secret after another."

"Saying what exactly?" Jrue asked.

"Are you sure you want to hear all of this?" I asked her. "It's... heavy," I warned.

She nodded slowly while releasing a long breath. "Just say it."

"According to my father, your father wanted a son *real* bad. He said that your mother didn't want to know the sex until she delivered, but having a son was all he ever talked about. And then she delivered two fraternal twin girls on the night she gave birth."

"So, me and her, and *not* me and Canaan," Cena said to me.

"I think my father was the one your mother talked to, Jrue, because he told me that an out-of-state adoption was supposed to be arranged, but he didn't have anything to do with it after the... switch."

"If my mother didn't give birth to Canaan, where the hell did he come from?" Cena questioned.

I shook my head. "He said he was the son of some dealer who already had mad kids and was struggling to put food on the table. So, he arranged for your father to pay him fifty racks for the baby."

Jrue interrupted me. "You're sitting here telling me that my biological father never wanted me and threw me away, far, far away from his view, while *she* got to go home and live a life he decided I wasn't good enough to?"

"I told you it was heavy."

"Is that all your father said?"

"For the most part," I said, leaving out how he'd gotten paid on the back end.

"I mean, it's his words against a ghost. It's not like I can ask either one of my parents. I can't imagine my mother even knowing this and being okay with it. She loved us both so fiercely. I just... it doesn't make sense," Cena replied.

"It was in the midst of our conversation that I started to think back to when I came to see you before the wedding, Jrue. You told me about your and your sister's DNA ancestry results, and then I discovered in Spain that you two shared the same birthday. It was a long shot, but it got me curious, so I had my brother find someone to look into it."

"What all did you find?" Jrue asked.

"I wanted all the birth, death, and adoption records of anyone born at Cranberry Hill Memorial Hospital on October 31, 1997. I found out a boy and a set of fraternal twin girls were all born within minutes of each other on Halloween."

"And did you find any adoption paperwork?" Jrue asked. "Or our birth records?"

"No adoption paperwork, but yes to the birth records. There was a copy of a birth certificate for Cena and Canaan."

"Nothing linking me to who I was born to?"

"No."

Cena interjected. "Do you think it was a legal adoption?"

"Nothing about any of this shit has been legal since the beginning," Jrue stated.

"I mean, what about the doctor or the nurses? Did no one speak up when they walked out of the hospital with a girl and a boy?" Cena asked.

"My guess is that they paid a lot more people off than just Canaan's real family," I said.

Jrue huffed. "So, this is all real, huh?"

Cena glanced at Jrue, who was clutching her hands and glancing at the doorway every few seconds. "Would you be open to doing another DNA swab with me? To prove it?"

My eyes widened when Jrue shot up from her position on the couch and tossed her hands up. "I'm sorry, but this is all too fast and too fucking much for me. I thought I could do it, but I can't. I'm not ready for any of this to be real."

"Don't walk away, Jrue," I convinced her. "Look, can we all take a minute just to settle down? I realize this is some heavy shit for both of you, aight? Just please, sit down."

Jrue shifted her glances around the room before crashing her body back down. "I'm sorry. Again, this is all new to me, emotionally, and I'm still all over the fuckin' place with it. Finding this shit out after all these years is a lot to sort through."

"I understand why you feel confused and hurt. Trust me; I still have a lot of questions too. I'm not trying to pressure or rush you into anything you're uncomfortable with. We can ease into this on your terms. Besides, I have a lot of things on my plate to figure out, especially when it comes to Canaan."

"What exactly do you mean by that?" Jrue inquired. "I mean, I know he's a piece of the puzzle, but just how important is he?"

Cena's chest puffed out with a sharp exhale. "I've been gathering all the evidence and proof I can against Canaan and plan to expose him to The Order, our family's organization."

"Expose him? For what? What did he do?"

"He went behind my back and arranged to take over as the head of our family when he knew our father chose me," she said, nostrils fat with anger.

"And exposing him will do what exactly? Make them put you in charge instead?"

"That's the plan. Right now, he's keeping his head down while planning and plotting. I was going to wait to tear him down until nothing was left, but what I found on him so far is nothing compared to what we unpacked today. He's not even my blood. There's no way he should have a say in our family's operations!"

"What exactly did you find?" I asked her.

"For starters, I found out he has a secret baby," she publicized.

I watched as Jrue's dark brown eyes went round. "What?"

"I hired a private investigator and had him followed. He's got a whole secret family out in Connecticut. He's got a five-year-old son with some light-skinned girl with red dreads."

"Wow," Jrue replied, crinkling her nose at the news.

Curiosity cocked my head to the side. "Why do you keep doing that?" I asked Jrue.

"Doing what?"

"Every time she says Canaan's name or mentions anything about him, you make a face," I pointed out.

"It's no reason."

Cena and I eyed each other before I placed my gaze back on her. "Jrue, if there's something you're not telling me—"

"It's nothing."

"It's something."

"Jrue, please," Cena emphasized. "All I want to do is make things right, the way they should be."

"Can you go back twenty-five years ago and do that? Because nothing has been right since then."

I blew air through my nostrils. "Jrue."

The corners of her eyes crinkled. "Okay. I do know something else about Canaan."

"What do you know about him?"

"How do you even know him?" I asked her, overriding Cena's initial question.

"The first time we met was when I was still working at Bliss. He was the nigga I went off on the night I quit because he got handsy with me in VIP."

I held up my hand to stop her. "Hold up. He put his fuckin' hands on you?"

"Relax. I handled it. Besides, I told you about it."

"You didn't say who the nigga was."

"None of that matters now because the second time his name started floating around was when my best friend showed me his photo."

"Yara?" Cena asked.

Jrue nodded. "Yeah."

"Why was she showing you a picture of Canaan?"

"Because... he's the father of her unborn baby."

Cena's eyes squinted. "What? S–she's pregnant?"

Jrue nodded reluctantly. "Yeah, she is."

"Does he know about the baby? Is she keeping it?"

"He does, and yes, she is, but they aren't speaking, and that's why it's important to me that whatever you have planned for him doesn't blow back on her. It's the only reason I said anything in the first place! I just want to make sure my friend is protected in all of this. Nothing can happen to her, okay? Nothing! Promise me that! Both of you," Jrue demanded, staring us both down.

Finding out that Canaan was the father of Jrue's best friend's baby didn't sit right with me, especially after finding out he'd put his hands on Jrue when I wasn't around, and there wasn't shit I could do about it. His true identity should have been a secret my father was tired of keeping, and I knew now that Cena knew the whole truth, she would make good on her word and take him down. If she didn't, I would.

"You have my word," Cena answered before me.

"Why should I trust you?"

"What other choice do you have? I know this doesn't mean much to you, but I'm not my father... *our* father."

"You're right. It doesn't. But what were they like? You know, *your* parents?" Jrue asked.

"My mother was great. Always nurturing, always made sure we knew we were loved. She died some years back."

"And your father?"

"He passed away recently."

Jrue cleared her throat. "Oh. I'm, uh, sorry for your loss. I don't know what it's like to lose a mother, but my father died a few years ago. So I know the void your heart carries."

"It's crazy we share the same DNA, and yet we're talking about two *different* sets of parents," Cena noted.

Jrue tipped her head forward in agreement. "I know. Even thinking about my relationship with my sister, Charity, is different now. I've always been used to being the big sister, and now, I might have been reunited with my *twin*."

"I think I would've liked growing up with a younger sibling instead of growing up alongside Canaan. He was a menace and still is. We never,

ever had that twin intuition shit you hear about, like Tia and Tamera. I just thought we didn't share that twin bond or that sibling connection, but now that I know what I know, it's all starting to make sense. Now more than ever," Cena admitted.

I sat amongst Jrue and Cena, listening to them talk about their different upbringings as children while reflecting on my own. It became clear that any relationship's core was love, not blood.

Seventeen

JRUE

CHARITY and I were spending some one-on-one time together in the nail salon. We sat side by side in hot pink royal throne chairs with our feet dipped in the bubbling water. She had her face buried in the salon menu while I tapped away at my iPhone screen, texting Kas. Since our unfinished conversation at his place, he'd asked me to pick a time when we could meet and finish it.

Kas: *We still on for dinner later?*
Me: *Yeah. I'll see you tonight.*
Kas: *Pick you up at eight.*
Me: *Okay.*

"You think I should get the chocolate spa pedicure or the lemon spa?" Charity asked, looking over at me.

"Does one bring you actual chocolate? Because if so, pick that and let me eat it because I'm starving."

She smacked her lips. "Um, no. And you still haven't picked where we're eating after this. You were supposed to be on your phone, looking something up."

"I know... I got a little, uh, sidetracked."

Charity snapped her eyes at me. "Mmhm. Who is he?"

A laugh found its way out of my lips. "What are you talking about?"

"I know that look."

"You're like twelve. What do you know about looks, Charity?"

"Don't insult me like that," she replied while rolling her eyes skyward. "And fine, keep your little boyfriend a secret."

"Trust me, nothing about him is little. His hands, feet, *everything* big," I revealed, spilling too much tea for her minor ears.

My heart was still all over the place when it came to Kas and the hold that he still had over me, but as much as I tried to hide it, my true feelings were broadcast all over my face. After speaking with Cena and getting the confirmation that the baby wasn't his and that their marriage was on paper only, I was open to seeing where things between us could go. As badly as I wanted to deny it, my heart was still rich with love for him. Having him along for the ride as I sorted through my family drama and identity had taken us to another level.

We let amusement flush through us. "I'm glad to see you smiling," she said.

"Yeah."

"How you been, though? With everything?"

My arms drooped to my side. Truth be told, I was still a thorny knot of emotions. "I don't know. It's still a lot. It's like I have a family, but at the same time, I don't have anyone anymore."

"You always got me. I don't care whose blood you have."

"No, I know that. Of course, I know that," I assured her. The truth hammered at my nerves before I spoke. "It's just this whole adoption thing is a blessing and a curse, for real. On the one hand, I just discovered that my biological father thought it was okay to leave me lying in the hospital with no one to claim me. And on the other, I'm like, thank God for Mama being childless at the time and wanting a baby so bad that she brought me home. The way she and Dad brought us up with so much love, staying up with us in the middle of the night, checking our closets and underneath our bed for monsters before bedtime, and kissing our boo-boos. I had a wonderful childhood. I never felt like I missed out on anything, and then, bam! Suddenly I'm being reunited with my long-lost twin sister."

A fine coat of empathy dusted her face. "I wish I never brought up getting that stupid DNA test in the first place."

"I know you feel like it opened a can of worms, and in some ways, it did, but it all had to come out sometime, right?"

"I'm glad you don't feel like you missed out on anything, but I still think they should've told you. I don't blame you for being angry at Mama. Hell, Daddy, too. I know I would be."

"I know. I'm trying to rise above all my negative feelings and focus on the positive."

"Good for you, sis."

I smiled. "Why, thank you."

"Now that we've gotten all the lovey-dovey ish out of the way, let's get back to the most important topic."

"What's that?" I quizzed.

"What the hell are we going to eat when we leave here?"

I snickered. "Okay, okay. Chill out. I'm looking now!"

* * *

HOURS LATER, I stared at my reflection in the mirror while trailing my eyes down the front of my black lace bustier top, matching satin mini skirt, and the strappy black heels laced up my calf muscles. That outfit, coupled with my poppin' curls and lip gloss, made me look *anything* but innocent.

A smile jotted across my lips as I placed my ear to the phone, answering Kas's call. "Yeah?"

"I'ma be pullin' up on you in like... three minutes."

"Okay, I'm ready for you."

"Mmm. I like it when you talk that spicy shit," he said with a soft chuckle.

I laughed. "Bye, Kas."

Eleven minutes later, Kas stood on the other side of the door with his smile hooked up on one side. "Three minutes, huh?" I teased.

His eyes traveled from my curls down to my three-inch heels before he licked his juicy lips. "Goddamn, you look—"

"Delicious?" I baited him with a smirk. "Oh, I know."

"I was going to say good enough to eat, but yeah, delicious works too."

"Thanks."

He stepped inside, narrowing the space between us. The smell of his cologne wafted past my nose, intoxicating me. "You should probably go change, though, unless you want me to have to body a nigga over you tonight."

I frowned. "Oh my God, shut up!"

"I'm serious, Jrue," he said with a face of stone.

"Well, niggas just gon' have to watch their backs tonight because I'm not changing," I informed him before grabbing my black blazer and clutch. "You ready?"

Kas followed me from my apartment and out to his car before opening the door for me. "Where exactly are we going for dinner?" I asked once he got inside.

"We have reservations at Thai Garden, that new upscale Thai restaurant downtown opening soon."

"Wait. Opening soon? You don't own this one, too, do you?"

He laughed. "Nah. I've never been before, but they are accepting limited dinner reservations from now until the end of the month, for their soft launch. They'll do their grand opening next month."

"Oh, so this is exclusive?"

"Yeah. I know some of the owners, and I've heard good things, so I figured we'd check it out together since I know we both like Thai."

One side of my lips curved into a grin. From one Thai food connoisseur to another, I appreciated how thoughtful he was being. "Sounds good."

We arrived at a brick building nestled in the corner downtown and got out. Kas held the door open for me, and I stepped inside, allowing my eyes to travel around the small eatery. The restaurant's ambiance was decorated with fresh flowers on the wood tables and floating crystals hanging from the ceiling. The soft candlelight, the low lighting, and the large pond made the whole place feel calm and romantic. Our table was beside the pond, allowing us to marvel at the tranquil waters while eating a delicious meal.

"I meant what I said in my apartment... about us starting over," Kas stated.

He'd wasted no time sparking up the conversation that had been weighing on both of our hearts. "I know."

"And now you're here, which means..."

"Which means I'm hungry," I replied.

"Stop fuckin' playin' with me, Jrue," he uttered just before the waiter approached us.

Kas ordered the lobster curry with egg noodles, and I decided on the pineapple chicken with jasmine rice. Once our waiter disappeared, Kas's dark brown orbs found mine. "I heard you when you said you ain't want me to push you to trust me. I understand I have to earn that back."

I rested my gaze on the calm water. "Good."

"Have you at least thought about it?"

"I have," I said with a quick nod.

"And?"

"And, if we do this, it has to go my way, on my terms."

He cocked his head to the side. "Terms?"

"Yeah."

"Explain."

"I liked your idea of us starting over from scratch, so we're going to take things slow, okay? Nice and easy."

"Is that all?"

"And I'm not fucking you again until *after* you're divorced," I declared, putting my foot down.

"That's fair, I guess. As long as no one else is touching you."

"Trust me, the only fingertips grazing this kitty are my own."

"What I tell you about talkin' that spicy shit?"

"Behave, Kas. We're in public."

"So? I know you said I can't put my dick inside you, but you ain't say shit about my tongue."

I clenched my thighs. "We're starting over right now! From scratch! Strangers again, okay?"

He bowed his head. "Aight, yeah. Cool. Nice to meet you. I'm Kas. What's your name, beautiful?"

His voice drew me inward while sending a chill down my spine. He'd taken me back to the very first time we met. "Jrue," I answered, "And it's really, *really* nice to meet you too."

FROM THE SERVICE to the food, everything was impeccable. Not once did I have to flag down our waiter for more water or anything else. Our meals and drinks were piping hot and flavorful, and the bill at the night's end was big enough to feed ten families in a third-world country for a few months.

"How you feel? You full? You sure you don't want to get some dessert to go?" Kas asked before we got up from the table.

"Trust me; I'm stuffed. These leftovers are gonna hit so good at like three o'clock in the morning."

Kas stepped up to open the door for me when a white man brushed past me, bumping my shoulder and knocking my to-go bag out of my hand.

"Excuse you!" I fumed.

"Fuck off!" He waved me off without even bothering to turn around.

Before a sound could escape my voice, Kas's boomed from beside me. "What the fuck did you just say?"

Hearing a more masculine voice made him spin around. "I said, fuck off!"

"What you need to do is apologize to my lady and pick up her mothafuckin food," Kas demanded while widening his stance in the process.

Hearing him call me his lady *and* bite a white man's head off inside an upscale restaurant sent a tingle down my spine. I usually wasn't a fan of the drama or making a scene, but I'd never been more turned on in my life. "It's okay, Kas. It's fine. Let it go."

"Nah, fuck that. I ain't lettin' shit go until he apologizes and picks your fuckin' food up off the ground," Kas responded before placing his hand on the man's shoulder, almost forcing him to kneel.

"Get your fucking hands off me! The bitch can pick up her own shit!"

His response did nothing but let us know which side he was on, and he'd stupidly chosen violence.

"I'ma tell you how this shit gon' go. Valet gon' bring my car around, and I'ma pop that mothafuckin trunk, and if you still runnin' that fat ass lip, I'ma put you on your knees and let you talk to my gun, aight? So you can either pick up my girl food, or you gon' really test my gangsta tonight and make me blow your white ass brains out in this mothafucka." He growled.

I reached out to place my hand on his shoulder, instantly realizing shit was about to hit the fan. "Kas, come on. He's not worth it. Let's just go."

"On your knees, mothafucka!" Kas directed. Everyone around us looked on in silence as the man got down on his knees and picked up my food. "Now put it in her mothafuckin hand and apologize."

"Here. I'm sorry."

"You what? Say it as loud as you was tellin' her to fuck off!" Kas challenged.

"I said I'm sorry!" he answered before placing my bag in my hand and running off.

Kas and I drifted outside to hear applause from people inside and the valet standing around who'd witnessed the whole ordeal.

"I'm sorry if I embarrassed you back there," he admitted once we were inside the car.

"You didn't."

"You sure?"

"He so deserved it."

"Hell yeah, he fuckin' did. Had to teach that racist mothafucka some manners."

"Do you really have a gun in the trunk?" I asked curiously.

"Not the trunk," he said, eyeing my seat.

"Wait, there's a gun in here? You were *really* going to shoot him?"

"If it came down to it. I don't tolerate too much disrespect, especially not behind you."

"Did you mean what you said when you called me your lady?"

"You been mine, Jrue. I told you I don't give a fuck if I'm married. I'm not lettin' you break up with me again."

* * *

KAS SEALED our whirlwind of a reconciliation date with a goodnight kiss before dropping me back at my apartment. I was still nervous about my decision to start over with him again, but there was a budding feeling of hope within me, and I was holding onto it with everything I had. My keys jingled against the lock before I stepped inside. My eyes instantly met with Yara, who met me with a smile.

"Hey."

"Hey," I replied.

"You look cute."

"Thanks."

"Hot date?" she quizzed.

"Something slight," I answered, noticing a little extra bling on her finger. "Is that an additional ring I see?"

Yara looked down at her ring finger and smiled. "Yeah. Nate and I eloped while you were away in L.A."

"Oh shit! Wow! Congratulations!" I beamed.

"Thanks. We announced the baby and our marriage to our families at the same time."

"Yeah? How'd they take the news?"

"They were overjoyed for us, especially our moms. They are already talking about baby names and wanting to call dibs on babysitting on the weekends."

I shot her a wide grin. "That's good to hear. They say it takes a village."

"Yeah, that's what I keep hearing. But how are you? I know you've had a lot of family stuff going on lately. Are you doing okay?"

I tipped my head forward, trying to find the best way to keep things as concise as possible. I felt like the news of my adoption was the new "hot topic" that everyone close to me had to know *all* the details about. But talking about it out loud helped me unpack and process it in some ways, I guess. And it was cheaper than therapy.

"I'm okay. It's heavy, but I'm learning to carry the load," I finally answered. "I know that I am loved and that I still do have a family, and I'm learning to be okay with that."

"I'm so proud of you. I mean, I can't imagine what you're going through."

I'd been holding back on telling Yara everything about my sit down with Cena and Kas. She'd moved on with her life and wasn't thinking about Canaan, and I didn't want to be the asshole who kept bringing up the ghost of her ex's past. Would she even care that Cena and Canaan weren't blood siblings since she'd married another man?

"Yeah," I murmured, still trapped in my thoughts. "I don't know. I lay awake at night and think about it sometimes, and I don't know if I could lie to my child about their identity like my parents did." The minute the words rolled off my tongue, I froze. "Oh shit."

Yara's face of concern turned into a frown. "Damn, Jrue."

My fingers touched my parted lips. "Oh my God, I'm so sorry! I wasn't trying to be shady!"

"No. I know you weren't," she said with a long sigh.

"All I'm saying is, my biological dad didn't want me, and my adoption was supposed to be an out-of-state arrangement, but then my mom stepped in. I'm so, so thankful for her for doing that, but at the same time, she and my father still chose to lie to me."

"Do you know if you were legally adopted?" Yara inquired.

"No. I haven't asked my mom since she confirmed it was true."

"Why not?"

"I don't know that it matters. Everything from the day I was born was illegal. Why should I assume any different for my adoption? As far as I know, she could've gotten paid off to take me," I stated, feeling myself going into a dark place.

"Are you going to talk to your mom again? And ask some more questions?"

I shrugged. "Yeah. I mean, I feel like I have to. The more I push against it, the more secrets come spilling out."

"Just be open, but also be prepared to accept disappointment, and try not to be too judgmental. We're only human, and who knows? The more you talk to her, maybe you'll find out she had a good reason to hide it from you."

"Thanks. I'll try my best. What about you, though? I mean, I know you're technically still a newlywed and all, but are you good? Are you happy?"

"I am," she stated with a quick nod of her head. "I *really* am. I feel like I made the best decision I could ever make."

Hearing her confirmation and seeing the glow of happiness in her eyes helped to settle my rambunctious nerves. Since the minute I looked down at her growing stomach, I could only think about Cena and what her tearing Canaan down would mean for Yara if shit blew back on her. We were finally back in a good space, and I wasn't about to say that I'd told Kasim and Cena about the true father of her baby, especially not finding out she'd eloped with Nate. I couldn't rob her of her moment. Besides, I figured carrying another life inside of her had to be stressful enough as is. She was living her life on her terms, and I didn't want to stress or scare her. All I wanted to do was keep her safe.

"Good. That's good," I said with a soft grin.

"Hey, I know we've got some time, but I wanted to let you know that I'll be moving out after the baby comes. We're looking into seeing if we can get a house built before then."

My mouth fell open in surprise as I playfully swatted her arm. "Wow. Okay! I see y'all doing grown-up things. Congratulations!"

"Nothing is set in stone yet. We're hoping to use his military benefits to help with the cost. You know all this shit is still new to me."

"You'll figure it out like you always do."

"Thanks. You ready to live alone? You know how you get during thunderstorms," she teased.

I smacked my teeth before letting out a soft chuckle. "I'm a big girl. I can handle myself," I assured her.

She rolled her eyes skyward. "Yeah, okay. How was your date?"

I shrugged while trying to stop my grin from turning into a full-blown smile. "It was... nice. The food was good. The live band was nice. We talked a lot."

"And?" she asked, expecting more than my sugarcoated details.

I huffed. "And we decided to give things another go."

Her brows rose in shock. "Wow, okay then. I see you doing grown-up things, too! Look at you going after what you want," she said with a round of applause. "Are *you* happy, Jrue?"

I didn't know why such a simple question felt so loaded, but it did. I quickly reflected on everything we'd been through in the months we'd known each other. Kas had made me laugh, moan, and cry. He'd made me feel feelings I never knew existed within me, so much that I wasn't sure happiness was the right word to describe what I was feeling.

"I'm hopeful," I replied.

Eighteen

CANAAN

Three months later

THREE MONTHS INTO MY BULLSHIT "LEADERSHIP" position, and shit hadn't gotten any better. I was exhausted as hell and restless at the same time. A nigga needed a come up so that I could make a comeback. But this time, on my own. If being a part of The Order had taught me anything, it was that you couldn't trust a soul, not even your own family. With the unending pressure and exhaustion of my situation weighing heavily on my chest, I felt more like a hamster on a wheel than a boss. I hated still not being able to move how I wanted to. I leaned forward, resting my throbbing head in the palm of my hand when the factory iPhone ringtone began to sound off. A huff of air pushed through my nostrils before I pressed accept.

"Who is this?" I asked, noticing the same number had called me two times already.

"Hello. My name is Jennifer Coleman with First Fidelity International Bank. I'm looking to speak with Mr. Canaan McQueen."

"This is him. What is this about?"

"I'm calling because your name was listed as a secondary contact on your father's business accounts."

I nodded, recalling I'd had things temporarily transferred into my name when my father became sick, and I took over his day-to-day operations. "Is there something wrong?"

"No. Nothing is wrong. This is a courtesy call. Any time a large transaction is processed by one of the account's authorized users, we make a courtesy call to let the primary contact know. But, since I couldn't get in touch with Mr. Silas McQueen, I called you."

"He's deceased," I informed her. "You can move me to primary."

"Okay, sir. I'll make sure to note that. And I'm sorry for your loss."

"Yeah. Thanks. Uh, can you tell me how much the transaction was and which account user authorized it?"

"Yes, sir. One moment," she said. I could hear her nails tapping away at the keys on her keyboard. "Okay, it looks like one million was moved."

"A million! By who?" I quizzed with my brows raised toward my hairline.

"By a Mr. Liam Morgan," she confirmed.

All I had to do was hear his name, and I immediately knew who he was. He was my father's business attorney who helped him set up different front businesses for us to wash our illegal money through. How did I not know about how much money was in that account? Either his white ass was extorting money from my family, or something else was happening.

I cleared my throat. "Thank you. And can you tell me the current account balance after that transaction?"

"No problem, sir. The total balance in that account is nineteen million-five-hundred and seventy-three thousand dollars."

My mouth instantly went dry as my heart sputtered in an uncoupled rhythm. "I'm sorry, you said nineteen *million*?"

"Yes. Nineteen million, sir."

"Thank you."

"Is there anything else I can do for you, sir?"

"Nah," I said with a devilish grin. "You've done more than enough. Thank you."

"My pleasure, sir. Thank you for banking with First Fidelity International Bank. Enjoy the rest of your day."

I ended the call, and my brain began to flood with an overwhelming amount of questions and assumptions that only aided and abetted my dysfunction. I could either continue to sit and draw my own conclusions, or get the truth straight from the horse's mouth.

* * *

I WHIPPED my car into the first parking spot I could find inside the dimly lit parking garage connected to Liam's office building and snatched my gun off the passenger seat. The elevator doors opened, and I marched inside the business suite filled with white men dressed in business suits. The entire space smelled like white privilege and cocaine. My eyes searched for Liam's name from one office to another until I saw it near a receptionist's desk.

"Excuse me, sir! Excuse me! Sir! Sir, you can't go in there!" The receptionist challenged my back as I swung open his office door. The glass frame rattled, threatening to shatter at my feet, but it held steady.

"We still on for dinner tonight at Barclay Prime? Yeah? Okay, I'll see you later, baby," he said into the receiver before his fearful eyes shot up at me. "Canaan? What the hell are you doing here?"

"Barclay Prime?" I quizzed. "The only person I know who loves to eat there is… my sister," I mumbled before my eyes darted over to the picture frame on the corner of his desk.

His eyes followed mine before he jumped up to try and swipe it away, but I got to it first. Looking down and seeing him and Cena holding each other and smiling with the sunset behind them blew my fucking mind.

"What the fuck is this!" I roared. "You fuckin' my sister?"

He held up his pasty white palms. "Canaan, just calm down, okay?"

"Are you fuckin' my sister, mothafucka?"

"It's more than that…"

"How fuckin' much more, white nigga? She's married, remember?"

"I know that. Please, just have a seat and calm down."

Irritated by his voice, I reached around and pulled my gun from my jeans. "I don't want to have a fuckin' seat. Start talkin', or I'ma start shootin' shit the fuck up," I warned.

"Okay, okay. W-what do you want to know?"

"Start with why the fuck you got a picture of you and my sister all hugged up and shit when she's married."

He cleared his throat. "Your sis... Cena and I have been seeing each other in-in-in secret for t-two years now. T-today's o-our anniversary," he confessed with ease.

I lowered my gun. "Now, was that so hard?"

His nostrils pushed out a sigh of relief. "Now, will you tell me why you're here? Because I know you didn't storm in here for that."

"Damn. You are a smart white boy. You're right. I came here to talk about why the fuck you took a million dollars out of one of my father's business accounts and why the fuck I didn't even know this account existed."

His eyes widened. "H-how did you know about that?"

"Don't worry about how the fuck I found out. All you need to be concerned with is that now that I know about it, you gon' make sure I get every fuckin' dollar in that bitch."

"W-what? Y-you want me to drain the account?"

"You heard what the fuck I said! Thought you could pull one over on *me*? That shit ain't happenin'! I want every single dollar!"

"Canaan, there's nineteen million dollars in that account!"

"And?"

"Think about it! Moving that much money all at one time would be a crazy red flag, and that's what we want to avoid. We both know that!"

"You just moved a million fuckin' dollars!" I reminded him.

"Yeah, from one business account to another. You're talking about draining it completely!"

I huffed. "What's the most I can get without raising any red flags?"

"The most? I don't know, Canaan. Maybe five at best," he shrugged.

"Million?"

"Yeah."

"How soon?"

"Canaan," he warned.

I raised my gun and aimed it at him again. "I said, how soon?"

"Two to three days... maybe?"

"Nah, I'ma need it faster than that."

"Maybe we can wire it... you know, into an offshore account. That would be quicker," he assured me with a head-bobbing nod.

"How much quicker?"

"I can set up a fake business account for you, but I'll need at least a day to get the paperwork drawn up and for everything to look legit before I can wire the money over."

"Where the fuck did all the money in that account come from anyway?" I asked, cocking my head to the side.

"From the art gallery... and a few other of your father's cover businesses."

"So, Cena knows about this account, too? She's known all along?"

"Yes," he confirmed before his eyes shifted downward.

"And you've been helping her move money around behind my father's back this whole time?"

His lungs pushed out a long sigh. "She knew how bad your father was with money and had me start moving things around."

"What does she plan to do with it all?"

"Talk to her about that," he insisted.

"Does she know you moved the million?"

"Yes."

"Why'd you do it in the first place?"

"Because she asked me to, Canaan! Just talk to her, okay? You two have a lot to sort out and discuss."

"What the fuck you talkin' about?"

"N-nothing. It's nothing. I didn't mean anything."

"You meant something."

"I didn't mean anything, okay? I-I've said too much already. Just talk to Cena, okay?"

"I'm talkin' to you! What all do you know?"

"Nothing!"

"You know what? Fine. I'll talk to her right here," I said, switching hands so I could pull out my phone and keep the gun trained on him simultaneously. I hit Cena's name, and the phone rang a few times before she picked up.

"Canaan? What do you want?"

"Oh, so I can't call my sister now?"

"We haven't spoken since a little after my wedding, and you know it."

"Fuck all that. That ain't the reason why I called."

"What?"

"I'm sitting here with your boy."

"My boy? What are you talking about right now? I don't have time for your bullshit," she griped.

"I'm sitting here with Liam in his office."

"W-what?"

"Yeah. He a lil nervous right now because I got my gun aimed at him."

"Canaan! Whatever you're thinking about doing right now, don't!" she warned.

"And what exactly do you think I'm thinking about? I mean, damn, sis, is the baby you're carrying your husband's or your secret lover's?"

"Canaan!" She hissed with ice in her tone. "What the fuck do you want?"

"I want to know about this secret account with over nineteen million dollars in it."

"You and I can talk about whatever you want. Just take the gun off of him and leave."

"Nah, because I know there's more to all of this shit. There's something nobody is telling me, and I'm not leavin' here until you do."

"I don't know what you're talking about."

"Then why the fuck does he keep tellin' me to talk to you? Huh? You tellin' me he's lyin' to me? Huh? You know what I do to niggas who lie to me, sis."

The line fell silent for a few seconds before I heard what sounded like sobbing on the other end. "I didn't want you to find out like this."

"Find out what?"

"I'll tell you once you've left Liam's office and he's safe. I'm not telling you shit until you leave!" she demanded.

I cut my eyes at Liam, who looked as if he was ready to shit himself. "Nice doin' business with you, white nigga. Call me when my shit is set up, or I'll be back," I promised him before storming out.

Neither Cena nor I spoke until the elevator spit me back into the parking garage, and I got back inside my car. "I left. Now speak."

"Are you in the car?"

"Yeah."

"Let me hear you start it up."

I smacked my teeth. "Come the fuck on, Cena."

"Start the fuckin' car, Canaan, and drive off!"

"Fine. I'm fuckin' gone. Stop draggin' this shit out and tell me what the fuck is going on."

Once again, the line fell silent, taking my aggravation to an extreme level. "Yo, Cena! Start fuckin' talkin', or I'ma swing back around that mothafucka!"

"What did he tell you?"

"He ain't tell me shit!"

"About us, Canaan. What did Liam tell you about us?"

"Y'all been dating for two years. Your husband know about that shit?"

"Don't worry about what he does or doesn't know. You know our arrangement is only business."

"You're right. I could give a fuck about Kasim or his bitch ass father!" I griped. His betrayal was a wound that still hadn't healed. "But business or not, if he doesn't know already, you gon' have a real hard time trying to keep up this charade when that baby of yours pop out half white."

"You really wanna sit here and talk to me about secret babies, Canaan?"

My brows raised. "I don't know w—"

"Don't even waste your breath trying to deny it. I know about *both* of your secret children."

Her words threw me for a loop so fast that I almost ran a red light. I slammed my foot on the brakes. If she had only mentioned knowing about one kid, I would've called her bluff, but the fact that she said two shook me. Yara hadn't crossed my mind in months, but she'd brought her to the forefront of my thoughts.

"How the fuck do you know about that?" I quizzed.

"Don't worry about how I know."

"I guess we both keepin' secrets, huh?"

"Yeah, well, I guess so." She agreed.

"Then tell me what else you're hiding from me, Cena. Tell me everything, or I swear to God I'll turn this fuckin' car around right now!" I threatened while gritting my teeth. She'd already knocked me off my square once. I wasn't going to allow her to do it again.

"Okay, okay. I'll tell you! Please, just keep driving!"

"Then start talking."

"I found out some things about us after Daddy died!" she yelled.

"Things? What things?"

"I don't know how else to say this, but... we aren't real twins, Canaan."

My brow creased. "What? What the fuck are you talkin' about, Cena?"

"We were born at the same hospital on the same night, but... that's all. We aren't related, meaning you aren't a McQueen."

My grip tightened around the steering wheel. "Fuck you mean I'm not a McQueen? Where the fuck did you get that bullshit?"

"It's the truth. Daddy paid someone for you because he wanted a son, but he got two daughters instead. So, he and Julius arranged for you and the original twin to be switched."

My ears were burning listening to her lies. They had to be. Didn't they? "Julius? Julius knows about this?"

"He does."

"I don't believe it."

"Then call and ask him. I have no reason to lie to you about any of it."

"If it's true, why haven't you gone to him yourself and tried to have me ousted from The Order, huh? Exactly! Because it's bullshit!" I denied.

"This is exactly why I didn't want to tell you! I knew you wouldn't believe it."

"Because it's not true! All you did was waste my time listenin' to this shit. Get the fuck off my phone!" I roared before ending the call.

My nostrils flared as I stared intensely through the windshield. My wheels started turning so fast that I could hardly keep up with all my wicked thoughts. If what she said had any truth to it, then why hadn't she used it against me already? Was she doing business with Julius since she'd married into his family, or was she lying to rattle my already battered cage?

I'd already thought to take the five million and run off to start my own empire with Trinity by my side. Aside from my son, she was the only joy I had. I was grateful that she still hadn't found out I hadn't filed the marriage papers. I knew that would be the straw that broke the camel's back for her. Either that or her finding out about Yara and the baby I'd put in her. If what Cena said was true, and I wasn't her biological twin brother, I needed all the true blood ties I could get. I had two heirs out there to claim and help me rebuild my empire brick by brick.

My chest heaved in and out as I pulled the car into a vacant lot. I clicked Trinity's name and waited for her to pick up.

"Yeah, bae?" she answered.

"Pack a bag," I instructed.

"What?"

"We leavin' the city in the next twenty-four to forty-eight hours. You, me, and Za."

"What the hell are you talkin' about right now, Canaan? You sound crazy."

"I'm fine. Just listen to what the fuck I'm sayin', aight?"

"Okay, baby. I'm listening."

"We gon' get the fuck outta here, and we gon' have a bunch more kids. I'ma be spillin' so much baby batter inside you, you gon' get sick of me!"

She giggled. "Are you serious right now?"

"Yes! We can go anywhere the fuck in the world you wanna go, aight?"

"Anywhere?"

"Anywhere!"

"Oh my God!"

"Don't tell me where it is right now. Just focus on packing up you and Za's stuff, aight?"

"This is so crazy, baby!"

I nodded. "I know. Just pack a bag and stay by the phone, aight? Don't make a move until I call you, aight?"

"Okay. I love you!"

"Love you too."

I ended the call and immediately sent Cena a text before calling Julius to get to the truth.

Me: *You might think you've got the upper hand in this, but ME AND MINE gon' come out on top in the end, bitch.*

The phone was one ring away from going to voicemail before he answered. "Canaan?"

"Yeah. It's me."

"What do you want?"

"I'm about to pull up on you, boss. We need to talk."

Nineteen

YARA

I'D OFFICIALLY BEEN a married woman for three months, and I hadn't gotten sick of the feeling. We'd started construction on our first house in Pittsburgh to be closer to his parents. Due to him working on base a lot, he missed most of my doctor appointments, but he seemed fine with the updates he got through me afterward. If the baby was doing okay, that's all he cared about, which was good enough for me. The fewer questions he asked, the better off we all were. Unbeknownst to him, I'd found out the sex of the baby a month prior and had been holding onto the secret until the timing felt more right. I sailed out of the doctor's office after my ultrasound appointment, with the envelope in my hand, when my phone began to ring.

"Hey, babe," I answered for Nate.

"Hey! How'd the appointment go?"

"Everything went well. Baby's heartbeat was good. Nice and high like it should be."

"Were they able to tell the sex today?"

"Yeah. I've got the envelope in my hand as we speak. I'm going to take it to the bakery now, and then my cousin will pick the cake up tomorrow and bring it to the gender reveal," I informed him.

"Bet. Are you excited?"

"Oh, yeah. You?"

"For sure. Ready to wear my blue for team boy!" he boasted.

"And what if it's a girl? You gon' trade in all that blue for some pink?"

"Guess I might have to."

"As long as you know. I don't want to be drying your tears in front of our guests," I joked.

"Shut up, girl. How are you feeling today?"

"I feel good. This trimester is treating me better than the first, so that's a blessing."

"Good. Well, I can't wait to see you later."

"Okay. Drive safe. Love you."

"I love you, too," he replied before hanging up.

* * *

AN ARCH FILLED with half-sky blue and half-baby pink balloons adorned the entrance to our gender reveal at my cousin's house. The tables were filled with finger foods and decorations that made guests pick a side, team pink or blue. The three-tier cake I ordered was sitting in the center of the table with blue and pink streamers as the backdrop. Once everyone arrived, Nate and I stood side by side and cut into each layer of the cake to discover the gender. The first layer was red velvet, causing everyone to boo. The second was vanilla, and the third was strawberry pink.

"It's a girl!" my cousin screamed while jumping into the air.

There was a roar of applause and a mix of screaming and cheering as everyone came up to hug and congratulate us. Nate pulled me into his arms and kissed my cheek. "Oh shit, it's team pink!"

I glanced up at him. He looked as if he couldn't wipe the smile off his face if he tried. His happiness was contagious, causing a grin to spread across my face. It was the picture-perfect moment. My smile faded when I noticed Cena standing by the exit with her hand on her very visible pregnant stomach, and I immediately felt a wave of anxiety wash over me. With a forced smile plastered across my face, I excused myself from friends and family and made my way over to her.

I parted my lips to greet her. "Cena, hi. Um, wow. It's been a while."

"Yeah, it has," she confirmed with a clipped nod.

"Pregnancy looks good on you," I complimented her.

"Thanks. You're glowing yourself. Congrats on the baby girl."

"Thanks. And you and Kas are having..."

"*I'm* having a boy," she answered, completing my sentence.

"Wow. Congrats to you, too. As you can see, Nate wanted a boy, but he'll have two of me to deal with instead."

Cena cocked her head to the side. "Two of you, or one of Canaan?" she asked.

My heart thudded to my feet, and I could've sworn I felt the ground shake. "W-what did you just say?"

"You heard me correctly."

"I don't know what you're talking about," I denied.

"Are you sure about that? Because I have reason to believe otherwise."

Feeling threatened, I stepped closer to her. "Look, I don't know what type of shit you're on, but this baby is *my* husband's," I said through clenched teeth.

"Look, I didn't come here to blow up your life."

"Oh yeah? Then why the hell are you here talkin' about some shit you know nothing about?" I quizzed with my arms pinned tightly across my chest.

"I came here to warn you."

My brows snapped together in confusion. "Warn me? Warn me about what?"

"Cena? What are you doing here?" Jrue asked, joining our conversation before Cena could answer my question.

She cut her eyes to Jrue. "I'm sorry, but I had to talk to her."

Jrue's voice heightened. "Talk to her about what?"

Instantly, I knew something was off. Why the hell were they talking as if they were old friends trading secrets? "What the hell is going on between you two, and why am I in the middle of it all?"

"Canaan knows, Jrue. He-he knows *everything*," Cena spilled.

My eyes cut a glare toward Jrue, reading her face while awaiting an answer. When I didn't immediately hear one, I asked, "What does Canaan know?"

Jrue shifted her attention to me. "Look, Yara. I told you bits and pieces of my adoption story, but there's more to it."

"How much more, Jrue?"

"Like... it's a high chance that Cena is my... twin sister," she confessed.

My eyes pinned her with a questioning glance. "What the fuck did you just say?"

"It's too much to explain right now, but long story short, Canaan and I were switched at birth, and he was raised as her twin instead of me. He's not her brother."

"Hold up. What? And what do you mean by high chance? Did you do a DNA test or not?"

"Not yet."

"So she could be anybody still." I huffed. "Look, Jrue, I know you're searching for your place in this world and all, and I respect the hell out of that, but all I'm asking is that you leave me the fuck out of it. Both of you," I told them before turning to go back to my guests that hadn't shown up to cause drama.

"Now that he knows who he isn't, I know he's going to run off, and when he does, he just might come after his child. After you," Cena warned.

Her cold words felt like icicles against my back. I spun around with my gaze tight on her. "What the hell did I tell you about saying that shit? Huh? He ain't comin' after nothin' because nothin' over here belongs to him!"

"Cena, just go. Okay? Now is not the time or place to talk about any of this," Jrue stated.

"Yeah. It really ain't," I fussed, ready to come all the way out of character on her ass.

"I knew showing up here today was risky, but I needed to talk to you. I know I told you I would keep her safe, and that's what I'm trying to do. She deserves to know there's a target on her back."

I jerked my attention back to Jrue. "So *you're* how she found out about Canaan and me in the first place? I don't know what type of sister-wife relationship you two have, but I'm not feelin' it! I can't believe you would go behind my back and share secrets that weren't yours to share!"

"I know that, and I'm sorry! I only told her to make sure you were protected!"

"Protected? Protected from what?"

"That's what I came here to tell you," Cena interjected.

"All the two of you have been doing is talking in circles about who knows what and who doesn't, and I'm tired of it. Either tell me what the hell is going on, or you can both leave!" I demanded.

"You need to run. Leave the city and get as far away as you can. I can help you and your man get out of here tonight on a private jet and some disposable cash to get you anywhere you want to go."

My heart rate quickened before a light chuckle escaped my lips. "Are you serious right now? This is all some sort of joke, right?"

Jrue's gaze moved to me. "I think she's *really* serious."

"Say the word, and I can make it happen," Cena replied.

"How much cash?"

"Five-hundred thousand."

My brows crept up toward my baby hairs. "Half a million dollars? To leave and never come back?"

"If I know anything about Canaan, he's manipulative and deceitful. He'll say one thing and then turn around and do another. If you want to raise your child on your terms, then I'm your best bet."

A breath blew thinly. "This all sounds crazy."

"I know."

"I need time to think and to... to process all of this shit."

"Time is of the essence, Yara."

"How much time do I have? I mean, we have family here and jobs. Nate is in the fuckin' military. What do you expect him to do? Go AWOL?"

"You have twenty-four hours max. Do you still have my number saved?"

I bobbed my head. "I do."

"Good. Use it. I expect to hear from you soon."

"Hold up," I said, stepping in front of her and grabbing her wrist before she could walk away. "No one, and I mean *no one* else needs to know about this conversation. Not your husband or your man or whoever he is. Not Nate and *especially* not Canaan."

"Yara," Jrue called out to me with urgency in her voice while frantically waving her hands.

I shook my head with frustration. "No, Jrue. I'm serious!"

"Who the hell is Canaan?" Nate's voice boomed from behind me. "And what don't we need to know?"

I froze. His questioning voice was like a gunshot to my chest. I quickly spun around to face him. His face was tight with rage. "Nate, I—"

"I'll give you two some time to talk," Cena interjected.

"No. Everybody stay right where they are and tell me what the hell is going on!" he demanded.

"Nate, baby! Lower your voice, okay? Please! Let's just go somewhere private and talk," I begged.

"No, fuck that. You need to tell me what the hell you three are trying to hide from me. What don't I know? Who is Canaan?"

"He's nobody," I assured him.

"If he's nobody, then what doesn't he need to know?"

I cut my teary eyes from Nate to Cena and Jrue, then over to my cousin standing off by the corner, silently watching my world crumble to pieces. I drew my attention back to Nate, whose eyes were burning with questions and rage. I knew I had no other choice but to come clean.

"This baby... she isn't yours," I admitted.

Nate's voice cracked. "W-what do you mean the baby *isn't* mine? Y-you cheated on me, Yara? Tell me the truth!"

"Yes."

His forehead puckered. "H-how many times? For h-how long?"

"I don't know."

"You don't know?"

"No! I don't know!" I alleged, feeling more ashamed as each minute skated by.

"With how many guys? Do you at least know the answer to that?"

I shot him a nasty look. "Yes, I know the answer to that! Don't disrespect me like I'm some two-dollar ho! I'm your wife!"

He sliced his eyes through me as if I was nothing but a whore and a fraud who couldn't raise a baby on her own, or maybe I was projecting my insecurities onto him. The baby wasn't biologically his responsibility, but as the woman he married, I felt like I still was.

"I don't know who the hell you are right now! Because the Yara I knew wouldn't lie to me like that! You knew all along the baby wasn't mine, didn't you? Didn't you!" he pointed out.

"Yes!"

"And you intentionally deceived me. You manipulated me... wasted my time. You're not a good fuckin' person, Yara. Good people don't do shit like lie and tell a man that a baby is his when you know it's not. They just don't do that to people."

I sighed explosively. "I was terrified, Nate! Absolutely terrified to tell you the truth because I didn't want to hurt you!"

He scoffed. "Yeah, well, looks like you did that anyway. If you respected me or any part of our relationship, you wouldn't have opened your legs to another nigga in the first place!"

"I'm sorry!"

"Who is this other nigga anyway? What's his name? Canaan? That's his baby inside you?"

I shook my head in protest, refusing to talk about him. "He's not important."

"Bullshit! He's the most important piece to this whole fucked up puzzle, Yara! You just think you can cut the head off a nigga and paste another one in its place, and shit is just supposed to work out?"

"That's not what I'm saying! Please, just hear me out, okay?" I begged him with pleading eyes.

His head wagged from left to right. "Nah. There ain't an excuse or explanation you can give me right now to make me trust you again. I'm out!"

I reached out for him, but he swatted my hands away. "Please don't leave me, Nate!"

"I can't be like you, Yara. I can't live a lie!"

My chin trembled as fresh tears slid down my cheeks. "W-what are you s-saying?"

"I'm saying I don't think I can forgive you for this, and if I ever do, it'll be a long ass time from now. But right now, I don't see us coming back from this."

"Listen, Nate! Listen to me! I know it will take time, and I know that forgiveness doesn't happen overnight, but please say we can work this out! You know as well as I do love makes a family, not just DNA. Just ask Jrue!" I said, tossing her right under the bus to save my own ass.

He darted his fiery gaze over to Jrue and then back at me. "This ain't about your friend! This is about you! You expect me to overlook your cheating mistake when it's bigger than that! It's not because you cheated, Yara! It's because you lied! Why the fuck would I want to be married to someone who would do some shit like that to me?"

The light went out of my eyes as moisture flooded my face. "If you loved me, you'd stay..."

"And if you *really* loved me, we wouldn't even be having this conversation right now," he said before storming past me.

"Nate! Nate, come back!"

* * *

FRESH TEARS PUMPED out of my eyes by the second as my cousin and Jrue cleared out all the guests after our debacle. I sat near the cake table, sulking and completely wrecked with pain. Seeing Nate cut and run like that had me fully expecting to be served with divorce papers first thing in the morning. A few minutes later, Jrue paced over to join me.

"Are you okay?" she inquired, placing her hand on my shoulder.

"Far from it."

"I'm so, so sorry," she empathized.

"I'm still mad at you." I hissed.

As betrayed as I felt by her for spilling tea she shouldn't have, I knew I only had myself to blame. I should've known it was only a matter of time before everything blew up in my face. Her facial expression was screaming, *"I told you so,"* at me, but her lips remained muted. She knew better than to kick me when I was down.

She cleared her throat before responding. "I know."

"Why didn't you tell me about your relationship with Cena?"

"I swear my intentions were all coming from a good place. I didn't want to stress you out; plus, you and Nate had already eloped. You'd made up your mind about everything. What was bringing up your past going to do but create more unwarranted chaos in your life? I was trying to avoid exactly what happened today."

I scoffed. "Yeah. I was too. But now my life is over."

"Don't say that."

"He's not coming back."

"Don't say that either."

"Why not? It's the truth. You were standing right there. You saw the look on his face, Jrue. He hates me for lying to him."

"He just needs time."

"Yeah, well, Cena made it clear time was something I don't have much of. What do you think I should do about Canaan? Do you think he's the loose cannon she painted him out to be?"

Jrue tilted her head to the side. "He may not be her blood brother, but she spent her entire life with him, so if anybody knows him..."

"It's her," I answered, completing her sentence.

"Yeah. What are you feeling like you want to do?"

I shrugged. "I don't know. A part of me doesn't want to leave or feel like I'll have to spend the rest of my life looking over my shoulder for a baby I didn't intend to create in the first place, but now... I don't feel like I have any other choice. Do you? Have you seen anyone present a better option?"

"No."

"Exactly."

"Cena's still outside... I think she's hoping for an answer before she leaves."

"Or maybe she's waiting around for you."

"What do you mean?"

"Are you going to do the DNA swab?"

Jrue's shoulders rose and fell. "I don't know."

"Stop pushing it off and just find out the truth already," I proposed.

She bobbed her head just as the venue doors creaked open. We both turned our attention to them to see Nate walking toward us. I shot up from my seat. "You came back!"

"Don't ask me why," he mumbled while shaking his head.

"Nate, please, sit down. Let's talk. I'll tell you everything. Anything you want to know."

"You can tell me from here," he replied, refusing to come near me.

Jrue looked at me. "I'll give you two some privacy."

Nate spoke up again once we were alone. "Look, I tried to listen to you, Yara. I really did. I tried to push all my reactive feelings and emotions to the back of my mind, but it didn't work, and I'm sorry for some of the shit I said earlier."

I blinked to freeze my tears in place. "Thank you for saying that. That means a lot."

"I just don't know that I'm ready to hear all the details right now."

"There are no big details, baby. It was casual. No feelings were ever exchanged between us whatsoever."

"Just bodily fluids," he griped.

I sighed. "It was my biggest, biggest mistake, and I'm so sorry."

"And you swear it was just him?"

"Just him."

"Does he know he got you pregnant?"

"Yes."

"You told him?"

I tipped my chin downward. "I did."

"*Before* you told me?"

"Y-yes," I admitted hesitantly.

Nate pushed out a long sigh. "I'm trying to understand why the fuck you lied to me in the first place. You were everything to me, Yara! I wanted to raise a family with you. I wanted *this* family with you."

"And we can still have that, baby. I promise you we can."

"I don't know about that. I don't know about anything anymore. You didn't just cheat while I was away, but you trapped me in a shitty situation. If I leave, I'm a shitty nigga. If I stay, I'm agreeing to raise another nigga's kid. I don't think it gets any more humiliating than that, and I don't know if my love for you is strong enough to get me through this."

"She offered me half a million to leave and never come back," I alerted him.

"Leave Philly?" he quizzed, snapping his brows together.

"Leave the state. Maybe even the country."

"Hold up. Half a million? What kind of cash cow are you carrying?"

I frowned. "This baby isn't a payday."

"Why did she offer you that much money to leave?"

"She said he's going to come after me once I have the baby."

"Come after you for what?"

"To try and take her from me and raise her himself."

"He would cut you out of the picture completely?'

"That's how she made it seem. Either that or kill me. I don't know."

"And you trust her? I mean, how do you know she's legit? How do you know any of this is real?"

My lungs flattened with a sigh. "I helped plan her wedding, so I was there when all those checks cleared. I know she's good for it."

"And what about him? You think she's tellin' the truth about him?"

I nodded. "I do."

"Then I think you should take the deal."

My eyes went round. Those were the last words I expected to hear come out of his mouth. "W-what?"

"Take the money, Yara. Take the money and go."

"Are you serious right now?"

"I'm dead serious. If it keeps you safe, you should go."

"What about our families? My job? The military? Are you willing to give all that up and come with me?"

"I said *you* should take the money and go, Yara. Not me," he clarified.

"I'm not leaving without you."

"You don't have a choice."

"What do you mean? Why don't I?"

"Because I'm not coming with you," he confirmed.

My hands began to shake as I choked back a sob. "Nate, please don't do this."

"I told you I'ma need some time to process all this, so this space will do us both some good."

"Space? What am I supposed to do in the meantime? What am I supposed to do without you?"

"What you've always done when I'm not around; live your life on your terms. And now, it's time I start doing the same with mine."

"Nate!

"Call me when you land and get settled so I'll know where to have my lawyers send the divorce papers, aight?" he stated coldly before turning to walk away.

"Nate! Please! Nate, come back!" I screamed while frozen in place.

Twenty

CANAAN

I LEFT Julius's house more confused than I was before I arrived. After confronting him about the bomb Cena dropped on me, he denied it all and tried to make me sound crazy for even bringing the shit to his attention in the first place. I didn't know which of their stories to believe, but I knew I didn't trust either one of them. As far as I was concerned, The Order was a sinking ship, and she could have whatever was left of it in my wake.

On my drive, I'd managed to arrange the perfect escape plan. I'd siphon money from Cena and her secret white nigga in exchange for his life, and after I got what I needed, I was going to go ghost. I had to start making the moves and decisions I needed to benefit the family I'd created and myself. Fuck the one I was or *wasn't* born into. I whipped into the parking garage and killed the engine. It was time to play the only card I had left to play. With Liam as my safety net, I only had to wait until the money hit my account before I kissed Philly goodbye.

My eyes prowled across the garage and landed on the elevator doors. I clenched my gun tight, waiting for them to open and for Liam to step off. Twenty minutes later, he came strolling out. As soon as he opened his car door, I ran down on him, allowing him to feel the cold steel of my gun against his temple.

"Move, and you die."

"C-Canaan." He stuttered while swallowing the rising lump in his throat. "W-what are you doing back here? I-I told you I'd work on setting up the a-account."

"This ain't about that."

He kept his head bowed. "Then what is it about?"

"Having a safety net, white boy."

"P-please don't do this! You're just re-reacting off of e-emotion! Please! I don't want any problems! I swear I'll get you the money!"

I glared at the pale man trembling in front of me before slowly trailing the barrel of my chrome pistol from the center of his chest to his forehead. "Oh, I know you will. Now, pop the trunk."

His shoulders remained tense. "W-what? Come on, Canaan, don't do this."

"I said, pop the trunk! Where the fuck are your keys?"

"H-here," he said, hand trembling as he reached inside his pocket to grab them.

I snatched them from his hand and jabbed the button to pop the trunk before pressing my gun to his spine and making his ass get inside. Liam lay curled up in the fetal position inside the trunk with his knees and forehead practically touching. He shot a pleading glare up at me as I bound his wrists and ankles with zip ties.

A whimper escaped his throat. "Please! Please don't hurt me!"

I looked down at him. His sandy brown hair was dripping with sweat. I grabbed a fistful of his hair and yanked his head back. We held each other's gaze for a second, and my mouth jerked to a grin. "Let's go for a mothafuckin ride," I told him before slamming the lid.

I hopped in his Benz and cranked the engine before fleeing the parking garage as quickly as possible to get far away from his office. Liam banged inside the trunk down the interstate, screaming until his voice was raw, for me to let him out and making me wish I would've duct-taped his mouth shut. Eventually, I pulled out my phone and called Cena when he went quiet.

"Canaan? What do you want?" she answered.

"I talked to Julius."

"And? Did he tell you everything?"

"Yeah, he did. And he ain't know shit about nothin' you told me earlier."

"What? Are you serious right now? He's obviously still playing games with you!"

"I don't know which one of you mothafuckas are playin' games, and I don't care, because I'ma make sure I get mine, aight?"

"What does that mean?"

"You'll find out soon enough."

"What?"

"I want five million wired to me tonight. I don't give a fuck where you gotta get it from."

"Who the fuck are you to demand anything from me?" she snapped.

"I'm the nigga who's got your fuckin' man tied up in the trunk."

"W-what?"

"Yeah. You heard me. Now like I said, you make sure I get that money, or I'ma put a bullet in your man's head," I threatened.

Twenty-One

KAS

JRUE CALLED me after her friend's gender reveal, and I could hear the angst in her voice. She wouldn't tell me what it was over the phone but said she was on the way over to tell me to my face. I hung up, not knowing what to expect when she arrived. Was it something about us or her friend Yara? I still couldn't believe she'd gotten herself tangled up with Canaan's irresponsible ass and was going to have his baby. I pushed those thoughts to the side when Jrue hit my phone, letting me know she was on her way up. One look at her when she entered, and I knew something was wrong. She was uncharacteristically jittery and utterly devoid of her usual charm.

"What's wrong?" I quizzed, eyes trained on her. "What happened at the gender reveal?"

I stalked forward before waiting for her to answer. Her body language alone told me she was touch-starved and needed a hug. Once she was safe inside my arms, she began to talk. "Everything went to shit, Kas. Everything."

"Tell me what happened."

She sniffled before pulling away. "Ugh, okay. Everything was going well at first. Everybody was happy when they found out she was having a girl, and then, bam! Cena showed up out of nowhere!"

"Whoa. Wait a minute. You said Cena?"

"Yeah, Cena. As in your wife Cena."

My brows snapped together. "What the hell did she show up there for?"

"I'm surprised you don't already know by now."

"What do you mean?"

"I'll get to that in a second. Let me get back to what happened after she showed up."

"Aight."

"Okay, so Cena shows up, and I see Yara step off to the side to talk to her. I played it cool for a bit, but I could tell by Yara's body language and the look on Cena's face that it wasn't a happy conversation, so I made my way over there."

"What were they talking about?"

Jrue sighed. "Apparently, Cena showed up to warn Yara that Canaan might try to come after her or the baby, and she offered her half a million dollars to run."

I shook my head. "She did what? Why does she think Canaan gives a fuck about whatever it is Yara is doing now?"

"She said he knows... the truth about the three of us, Kas. And she said he's crazy and unpredictable, so she showed up to warn her."

"What did Yara say? Did she take the money?"

"I don't know what she's going to do. When I left her, she was talking to her husband. And that right there is a whole other shit show," she disclosed.

"What happened with that?"

I watched her pull in a tight breath before her chest flattened. "He walked up to our conversation and overheard Yara mention Canaan's name. I tried to fuckin' stop her from talking when I saw him coming over to us as subtly as I could, but she just kept going!"

"Damn."

"So then she had to tell him the truth. Like, the whole truth about her cheating with Canaan, the baby not being his, all that. It was so, so terrible," she said while wagging her head from one side to the other.

"Hold up. She was trying to pin Canaan's baby on another nigga?"

"Yeah," Jrue admitted.

"Damn. She wild as fuck for that one. That's fucked up."

"I know, I know. I was doing my best not to say I told you so. I swear it was like the *worst* fuckin' day ever. I felt *so* bad for Yara. He stormed out of there enraged, and she was crying her eyes out. But he *did* come back after we cleared everybody out, so maybe they worked it out. I don't know. I'll talk to her when I get home."

"Damn, girl. That shit does sound stressful as hell.

"And I've got the matching headache to prove it," she griped. "But there's still more I haven't gotten to yet."

My brows rose and fell. "Goddamn. How much more happened there?"

"I talked to Cena again after the gender reveal, and she told me more about her and Canaan. He really *is* crazy."

"I already knew that. What exactly did she say to you?"

"She's been working with her man to move money around for different businesses, and Canaan found out about this secret account with a lot of money."

"How much money?"

"She said over nineteen million."

My brows jutted toward the ceiling. "Oh shit."

"And she told him about them not being blood-related, but he didn't believe her. All she kept saying over and over was how crazy he was."

"Did she seem scared?"

Jrue shook her head. "She didn't say she was."

"But did she look it?"

"I could tell she was worried," Jrue confirmed.

I drew in a long breath before pulling her in for another hug. "You sound like you had a long ass day."

"I told you I have the headache from hell to prove it."

"Let me cater to you."

Her forehead creased. "How so?"

"First, I'm going to draw you a nice, warm bath. Then, fix you a drink. And lastly, I'ma give you somethin' to knock that headache right out of you."

"I'm not fuckin' you. I told you that," she rehearsed.

"I ain't say nothin' about dick. That was all you."

She smacked her lips. "Whatever."

"Get your mind out the gutter, nasty," I teased, which brought a smile to her face.

"So, you down for this catering session, or nah?"

Jrue made sure to roll her eyes before agreeing. "Okay, fine."

I scooped her into my arms, carried her upstairs to my bedroom, and laid her across the bed. "Lay here while I go draw your bath water," I insisted.

When her water was ready, I stalked back over to the bed and peeled off her clothes layer by layer until there was nothing left. I dipped her body inside the tub and allowed the water and bubbles to touch her in places I couldn't for the time being.

"The temperature feel okay?"

"Feels great," she confirmed.

"Good. Try your best to relax."

"I can't remember the last time I took a bubble bath."

"Yeah?"

"Mmhm..." She uttered before pulling her hair up and closing her eyes before relaxing her head against the rolled towel I had cradled behind her neck.

"I'ma let you chill for a bit while I go get you that drink," I told her before leaving her alone with her thoughts. Before returning, I jogged downstairs to grab her a bottle of water and two Tylenol. "Here you go."

Jrue looked at the bottle of water and then up at me. "When you said drink, I thought you meant something... *stronger.*"

"Nah."

She side-eyed me. "I know just because I let you undress me, you think you gon' fuck."

Her assumption made a soft chuckle escape my lips. "That's what you think I think, huh?"

"Aren't you?"

"Nope."

"Yeah, okay," she said before tossing the pills down her throat and taking a swig from the water bottle.

"Sit up and let me get your back."

She leaned forward, making slight waves in the water before speaking up. "I agreed to get the DNA swab with Cena," she confessed as I washed her back.

I stopped for a moment to look at her. "For real?"

"Yeah."

"And how do you feel about that?" I quizzed.

"I mean, I know I was against it at first, but it's like, the more I push all of this off, the more our webs interconnect. At this point, knowing the truth is better than living in denial like Canaan."

"Yeah." I agreed. "You're right about that. When you gon' do it?"

Jrue raised her arms skyward before stretching her body. "We haven't set a date yet, but soon," she told me. "We're just going to rip the Band-Aid right off and do it."

I stared at the suds and water sliding down her nipples and looked away before my dick turned to a brick in my pants. "You ready to get out yet, or do you wanna stay in here until your fingers prune?" I quizzed, changing the subject.

"I'm ready."

I grabbed a towel and wrapped it around her body as she stood. Jrue held it tight to her body and stepped out of the tub, one foot after the other. We walked into my bedroom, and she looked down at her pile of clothes on the floor. "Damn. I don't have anything clean to put on."

"You don't need anything."

She snapped her neck back at me. "See! I told you! I knew it!"

I walked over to her, diminishing the gap between us. "I said I wasn't thinking about fuckin' you. I ain't say I wasn't thinkin' about eatin' your pussy."

"Kas—"

I cut her sentence off at the head. "Don't make me beg for it, Jrue, because I'm not a please type of nigga," I stated before pulling her towel down to the floor.

I wrapped my hands around her waist and placed her back on my bed before burying my head between her soft brown thighs. Jrue rested her back against the sheets, balling them up in her grasp. "Oooh shit." She purred as her legs spread like butter for me.

I let my tongue game lull her to sleep and then went back into the bathroom to shower and wind down. Twenty minutes later, I stepped out of the shower and wrapped a towel around my waist before stepping over to the mirror. I smeared my hand across the mirror, wiping away the fog so I could see my reflection. My hand traced down my wet beard before my phone vibrated on the sink's edge.

"Hello?" I answered for Cena.

"Ka-Kasim! I-I need help. Canaan. It's Canaan—he–"

"He what, Cena? Are you okay?"

"He's got Liam! He kidnapped Liam!"

I gripped the phone tighter. "He what?" I growled.

"He wants five million dollars, or he's going to kill him, Kasim! Canaan is crazy, and I know he will! I know he'll do it! He fuckin' hates me! Now more than ever!"

"Okay, aight. Calm down, aight?"

"I can't! I can't have this baby without Liam, Kasim! I can't do it!"

A frustrated sigh pushed through my widened nostrils. Cena was seven and a half months pregnant and still had weeks until her due date. I couldn't have her stressing out over that goofy ass nigga Canaan.

"Look, I need you to calm down and listen to me, Cena. Aight? Can you access that much money quickly?"

"Not without Liam, but maybe I can make him think I can. I-I don't know. I can't fuckin' think straight right now!"

"Jrue told me he found out about some secret account," I informed her.

"He did, and Liam told me he was working to set up an account for him to move some money. I knew he was planning to run, you know? But when Liam didn't show up for our dinner reservations, I started to get worried. I was about to track his phone when Canaan called and told me he had him. I-I need you to-to help me k—"

I clipped her sentence. "Say less. Send me your address and stay where you are. I'm coming to you."

"O-okay."

"And Cena, I know this goes without saying, but try not to stress, aight? We gon' get him back."

I hung up, more excited than enraged. I'd wanted all the smoke with

Canaan's ass ever since I found out he'd put his hands where they didn't belong when it came to Jrue. Fucking him up would be the icing on the cake and the cherry on top for me.

After throwing on some clothes, I went back to the bed and gently began to shake Jrue's shoulder. "Wake up, beautiful. Wake up."

She stirred in her sleep before slowly cracking open her eyes. "What? What's wrong?"

"I wanted to let you know I'm leavin'. I gotta go."

She sat up on her elbows, still a bit disoriented. "What? Go where? Why?"

"I gotta go."

"Damn. I don't even remember falling asleep," she said with a yawn.

I smirked. "Because my tongue put that ass right to sleep."

"Shut up. Tell me where you're going."

"I'll be back. Go back to sleep. I'll be back."

"Tell me," she demanded.

"I don't want to scare you."

"So don't."

"It's Cena. She said Canaan kidnapped her man and is holding him for ransom. He wants five million dollars," I shared with her.

"Oh my God!" she said, covering her open mouth in shock.

"Yeah. So, I'll be back."

"No. I'm going with you," Jrue insisted before hopping out of bed.

I held my hands out to stop her. "Nah. You gotta stay your ass right here where I know you're safe."

"No, Kas! I'm going with you!"

I clenched my jaw, unwilling to argue with her because I knew how pressed for time I was. "Fine. Throw on something, and let's go."

I sailed through one traffic light after the next. Once we'd been in the car for a few minutes, Jrue twisted her neck in my direction.

"Where are we going?"

"We have to make a stop first."

"Where?"

"You'll see," I told her, glancing in her direction for a split section.

Ten minutes later, we were pulling into the back entrance of the building she'd helped decorate.

"Wait. Why are we here?" she inquired when I killed the engine.

"Come on."

We got in the elevator, and her eyes widened, watching my finger jab the PH button for the penthouse. "I thought you said I couldn't go up here."

"That was before."

Jrue rested her eyes on me. "Before what?"

My gaze aligned with hers. "You became mine."

"What's up here?"

"You'll see in a minute."

The elevator chimed, and I stepped ahead of her onto the tarped floor. "Watch your step," I warned her before reaching for her hand.

"What the fuck is all this?" she asked, following me into my weapons room and looking around.

"This is what I do," I told her.

Her eyes skated from the various machine guns, Uzis, Desert Eagles, and AK-47s adorning my walls. "Are you going to kill Canaan?" she questioned.

"Yeah."

I met her questioning look and watched it turn into a brave gaze. "Which one are you going to use?"

I rested my eyes on the Beretta with my silencer attached before pulling it down. "This one. Gotta be quick, in and out," I stated.

"Okay, then. Let's go."

"*We* aren't going anywhere," I corrected her.

Her long lashes flew high. "What do you mean?"

"I can't have you there."

"No! I'm going with you!" she protested.

I let out a frustrated breath before reaching out to grab her wrists. "Jrue, I have to—"

"Go burn the world down?" she asked, cutting me off. "I know."

We both knew I didn't have time to stand around and tell her exactly what I would do or where I would do it. She just couldn't be around any of it. I wouldn't allow it. "Okay, then you know that I can't have you anywhere around that shit. I won't be able to think fuckin' straight, and I need all my energy devoted to this."

She sighed. "Okay."

"I'll be back. Two hours, max."

"Promise?"

"I do."

"Come back to me, Kas," she instructed softly while gently stroking my beard.

I reached out to grab her hand and kissed it. "I will."

"In one piece," she clarified.

"Every last piece," I promised before kissing her goodbye.

* * *

CENA and I pulled up to the rooftop of the car garage connected to Liam's office building. "That's it! That's Liam's Mercedes over there!" she pointed.

I drove over to it and whipped into a spot a few spaces down from them. Once Canaan exited the car, I got out, and then Cena got out too.

"Stay behind me," I told her.

"Where is he, Canaan?" Cena yelled. "Where is Liam?"

Canaan rolled his eyes before popping the trunk. "He coolin'. Still breathin' for now."

"No! Get him out of the trunk! I want to see that he's okay with my own eyes," Cena demanded.

"I want to see my fuckin' money."

"I got the bag. Now go get him!"

Canaan walked around to the trunk and pulled him out. Liam's body hit the ground with a thud, and Canaan dragged him around the car by his hair so we could see him.

"Oh my God! Let him go, Canaan! Let him go right now!" Cena ordered.

"Cena, chill," I warned her. "You need to calm down!"

Cena held out a black duffel bag filled with cash. "Here's half a million in cash! It was all I could get last minute. Liam will wire the other four and a half million to you once I get him out of here, and I can make sure he's safe."

"Bitch, you think I was born yesterday? Ain't nobody leavin' here until I get my full five million."

"All I need is my phone," Liam announced. "J-just undo my wrists, and I can finish doing everything from my phone."

"How do I know you won't do some slick shit like call nine-one-one or somethin', white nigga?"

"I won't! I swear to God I won't. Just, please! Give me my phone, and you'll have your money!"

Cena and I stood back while Canaan cut the zip tie around Liam's wrists and fished his cell phone out of his pocket. "You got five minutes." Canaan growled, aiming the gun at his head.

We stood by silently, watching Liam click away at his screen. "Done. I finished the paperwork for your business. Now I can transfer the funds. Give me one minute. Okay. Done. See. Look at the screen. The money has been transferred!"

Canaan looked at the screen and smiled before reaching down to pick up the duffel bag.

"You got your money, nigga. Now let him go," I barked.

He cut the ties around his ankles, and Liam ran over to Cena. They hugged before jumping inside Liam's car. She locked eyes with me before speeding off, leaving the two of us alone for me to handle my business.

Canaan stepped off when I called out to him. "Hold up, nigga. We got more to discuss."

He frowned. "We ain't got shit else to discuss."

"Oh, I think we do."

"I don't give a fuck what you think, nigga. I said, I ain't got shit to discuss with your ass." He uttered with a scoff before walking away from me.

"Guess I gotta jog your fuckin' memory then, nigga," I stressed before hauling off and landing a punch across his jaw.

He charged at me, knocking my gun out of my jeans as our bodies thudded against the ground like a ton of bricks. I quickly rolled over and hovered over him, landing one blow after another to his face. I promised myself I'd savor each second of going to work on his ass for touching Jrue, but I couldn't hold back once I started. I couldn't take my time. I couldn't slow the fuck down or even imagine pressing pause on my twisted version of fun. All I saw was red, and I bashed his face until blood leaked everywhere. It was then that I drew back to assess the damage.

Canaan was crouched into a tight ball, trying to shield his face. From what I could see, my fists had turned his right eye eggplant purple, and it was sealed shut. The cuts and scrapes across his face were raw and oozing with crimson blood. I stood to my feet, ready to leave him lying in pain.

"You had enough, bitch nigga?" I quizzed before drawing back and kicking him in the stomach.

He spat blood onto the floor before tearing his eyes to mine. I walked over to pick up my gun and stood over him as he hugged his ribs. I squeezed the trigger twice without a second thought or a drop of mercy. Enjoyment spread my lips into a sinister smile as I watched the bullets leave the chamber and enter his chest. Light, gasping noises escaped his lips as his eyes turned fearful. He knew it was the end. I watched the life leave his body before I lowered my arm. If my father taught me anything, it was never to be afraid to kick a nigga when he was down. I pulled out my phone and called my father's men, who were on standby, to clean up the mess, before grabbing the duffel bag full of money, getting inside my car, and speeding off.

* * *

I RETURNED to the penthouse where Jrue was to find Cena and Liam there as well. The minute the elevator doors parted, Jrue raced over to me. Her eyes noticed the blood stains on my shirt, and she reacted before I could say anything.

"You said you'd only be two hours, Kas! Two!" she scolded me.

"I know."

"There's blood on your clothes. Are you hurt?"

"I'm good. All I need is a shower."

"Are you sure you're okay?"

"Yeah. I said I was good. Damn. You were worried about a nigga, huh?" I teased.

She smacked her lips. "Just give me a fucking hug," she demanded before crashing her body against mine.

I kissed her forehead. "I'm gonna take a shower, aight? I'll be back."

"And for the record, I wasn't *that* worried about you, nigga. I was just... wondering where you were."

I scoffed with a slight chuckle. "Yeah, aight."

I stepped off to shower and change clothes before joining the three of them back in the main area.

"Kasim, can we talk?" Cena asked while walking over to me with her hand cradling her belly.

"'Sup?" I questioned just as my phone dinged. I glanced down to see a text from one of my father's men, letting me know that Canaan's body had been properly disposed of and the scene had been wiped.

"I just wanted to say thank you... for everything," she said.

I shrugged. "It ain't a problem."

"With as much as you've done for me, and as grateful as I am, I need you to do one more thing for me..."

My head leaned to the side. "What's that?" I inquired, shifting my weight from one leg to the other.

"I need you to set up a meeting between your father and me, and I need you to do it soon."

"Why the fuck would you want to meet with my father after knowing all he's done?"

"I want to make a new deal with him."

"What kind of deal? You know you can't trust my father."

"I don't have to trust him, at least not right now."

"What do you mean?"

"If he wants Douglass Simms to take over, I'll *pay* for my family's spot back in The Order and my rightful place at the head of the McQueen family table, like it should've been before all this shit happened."

It was then that I saw exactly why Silas wanted his daughter to take over for him. Cena was nothing less than a boss and nineteen million dollars to the good. And money spoke volumes to a man like my father.

"Bet. I'll set it up," I told her.

"Thank you. And once we do this, there will be no need for us to stay married anymore. We can end this and officially go our separate ways."

Cena had said the words my ears had longed to hear for months. "I think Jrue would appreciate that."

She chuckled. "Yeah, Liam, too."

Twenty-Two

KASIM

FROM MASERATI'S TO MERCEDES, my father's driveway was lined with luxury cars from all The Order's family heads. I knew they would be congregating in one place for their meeting, so instead of setting up a one-on-one between Cena and my father like she'd asked, I decided it would make more of a statement to not only attend The Order meeting, but completely crash it.

I jabbed the doorbell before glancing over at Cena. "You sure you ready to do this?"

"Ready as I'll ever be. I'm about to drop this baby in a month. It's now or never."

"Aight, then," I told her. "Let's do this."

The door opened, and we stepped inside to see the Rivera, Massey, and Palmer families in attendance, and Xavier Underwood, Janessa's father, who had survived the shootout at Cena's father's funeral. Soon after, my father cascaded down the grand staircase with the tips of his middle finger and thumb kissing to form the letter O and holding it over his heart. Like clockwork, every one of us returned the gesture in silence. It didn't take long for his eyes to land on mine, and then Cena's.

He marched over to us. "What are you doing here right now, Kasim?"

"I suppose my wife's invitation to tonight's meeting got lost in the mail."

"Excuse me?"

"Canaan is dead, Pa," I informed him.

"And I, as the rightful heir of the McQueen family businesses and legacy, am here to make you a deal," Cena interjected.

My father's head tilted to the side with intrigue. "Oh?"

"Yes," she said, holding her belly. "I know your relationship with my father was... troubled. But I'm not here to waste your time, Julius."

"I'm listening."

"My husband told me that you plan to have Douglass Simms take over the McQueen family spot in The Order. Is that true?"

He shot his eyes over at me before slowly dragging them back to her to answer. "Yes."

"And yet, when I look around your beautiful foyer, I don't see him or any of his men."

"It's not official yet."

"Good, because it doesn't need to be."

"And why is that?"

"Because I'm here to pay off my father's debts and pay for my family's spot back in The Order and my rightful place at the head of the McQueen family table, like it should've been from the beginning. And I will do without the hyphenated last name of Barnes attached to mine."

My father took one look at her before pushing out a nasally chuckle. "Mmm. I think we both know you're biting off a lil more than you can chew."

"How much does my father owe you, Julius? And you, Ruiz?" Cena asked, expanding the conversation to anyone in earshot.

"A lot more than I think you're willing to pay," my father answered.

"Give her a number, Pa," I added.

I studied my father closely as he traded glances with Ruiz. It was as if they were secretly coming up with a suitable number for them that would seem astronomical to her.

"Fifteen million."

"And that's everything? All his debts, and everything?"

"That's all."

Instead of responding to him directly, she placed her attention on her phone, tapping away at the screen for a few seconds. "Done," she said, shooting her eyes up at everyone.

The room fell silent as my father's forehead and every other nigga in there bunched up in confusion. "What?"

"I said, done. Fifteen million was just wired to you. You and Ruiz can figure out the split later. It was nice doing business with you. I'd love to stay for tonight's meeting, but this baby simply does have me exhausted, but I'm sure I'll be hearing about the next one, right?"

I watched my father's lips twist to the side. He was pissed, but he had no other choice but to see her as the boss she was. "Right."

"Great. Oh, and do me a favor, will you? Tell Douglass Simms he's got twenty-four hours to vacate *my* territory, or I'll spray him and all of his men like bugs. Thanks," she replied before walking out.

Twenty-Three

JRUE

IT HAD BEEN two weeks since Canaan's death. Between work and Kas, Cena and I found time to do the DNA swab earlier in the week, and I'd been battling my feelings about it ever since. I was going to meet with her to go over the results, when Yara called.

"I miss you," I whined before huffing out a sigh.

"He finally did it! After keeping me on pins and needles for two fucking weeks, that bastard finally decided to send over the papers to have our marriage annulled!"

My eyes bugged, and my neck snapped straight. "Oh shit."

She began to sob into the receiver. "I can't believe he *actually* did it."

My lips twisted to the side, careful not to say the first thing that came to mind, which was, *bitch, do you really blame him?* She'd been playing a game for two, knowing there'd been *three* people involved. Had he cheated on her and asked her to accept a baby he'd created with some other bitch, she would've told him to go straight to hell with turn-by-turn directions on how to get there. But at the end of the day, she was my girl, and I would remain in her corner, period.

"I'm so sorry, Ya-Ya. I mean, do you think he's just still reacting off of anger? You don't have to sign right this second, do you?"

"No, but I don't think he will change his mind about this."

"You sure? I mean, I know you fucked up, but one fuck up doesn't erase all the history you two have, right?" I inquired, trying to lean on the brighter side of things.

She pushed out a long sigh into the receiver. "His reason for the annulment was that our marriage was based on fraud, Jrue. Fuckin' fraud! He's not turning back on shit. Besides, who needs love when you can have money?"

"Wait. What do you mean?"

"He knows about the money Cena offered me to leave, Jrue. It's not like we had any sort of prenup. What if he tries to take it all from me? What the fuck are me and my baby going to do then?"

"Oh shit. Do you really think Nate would be that petty?"

"I completely obliterated that nigga's pride, girl. I almost think he reserves the right to be as petty as he wants to be. And even if he doesn't, I'd rather just be prepared for anything upfront. I'll tell you one thing. I'll never trust another nigga for as long as I live."

I frowned. "Don't say that, Yara. I know it's bad now, but you've still got a lot to look forward to. And I mean, the problem you were running from is gone. You can always come back home. There's still a whole vacant side of the apartment waiting for you."

The line went silent for a few seconds, causing me to speak up again. "H-hello?"

"I'm here," she answered.

"Did you hear me?"

"Yeah."

"And?"

"I don't know if I want to come back. Cena may have shown up at the wrong fuckin' time, but at the same time, without her, I would still be in Philly hiding under the covers with the blinds shut because I don't want to face my family or his. I just can't. I'm too fuckin' embarrassed. Plus, I don't want to be around people and hear everyone's mouths about where I went wrong and how they would've handled things if they were in my shoes. Maybe I'm just... better off staying where I am, at least until the baby comes," she vented.

"You have people here who still love you, and the last thing you're going to want to be when that baby comes is alone. A little help is better than none at all," I reminded her as I pulled into a parking spot and killed the engine. I unhooked my seat belt but continued to sit in the car and talk to her.

"I hear you, girl. I do. I just need to stay away long enough to clear my mind, you know? When I bring this little girl into the world, I can't be in this same fucked up mindset."

"You're right. Well, just know I'm here for you and giving you the tightest, warmest virtual hug ever right now, okay?"

"Thanks. You about to go?"

"Uh... yeah. I'm, um, meeting with Cena in a minute."

"What, why?"

"We did the swab," I informed her.

"And? Is she your sister?"

"I don't know yet. We agreed to read the email together when the results came in."

"Wow, okay. Well, are you okay?"

"Yeah. I'm okay. I won't ask if you're okay because..."

"Yeah. Don't."

"I'll call you back, okay?"

"You better. You know my ass will be glued to the phone, waiting to hear this tea."

I let out a soft giggle. "Yeah, okay. I love your crazy ass."

"Love you more," she replied before hanging up.

I slid my phone inside my purse before stepping out of my car and making my way down the block and into the brick establishment. My eyes locked in on Cena, and I drew a deep breath, refusing to release it until I got closer to her table.

"Hey, Jrue," she greeted me.

"Hey."

"Please, have a seat. Are you hungry?"

"No appetite," I said while shaking my head.

"Yeah, no. I get it. I'd been sitting here for like ten minutes, so I got the waitress to bring us some water."

"I'm sorry. I was sitting in the car on the phone talking to Yara."

"How is she?"

"She's... she's going through it, but I think, I hope, she'll pull through it all a better person in the end."

"Listen, I know that's your friend, and she's a nice girl. So, I want you to know that even though Canaan is gone, I've put some money aside in a trust for his son *and* your friend's daughter."

"Wait, Cena. You what?"

"I don't know if this baby is softening me up or what it is, but if we were to rewind to a few months ago, I would've thought those children were my blood niece and nephew. Just because their father was a menace doesn't mean they'll be. I just... I don't know. I just wanted to do my part and ensure the kids were good at the end of all of this, so I sent some money to his baby's mom and got Yara out of harm's way."

"I want her to come back, but I don't know that she wants to. Do you think it's safe right now?"

"I don't see why she couldn't, but if she doesn't want to, she doesn't have to right now."

I sighed. "Thank you... for staying true to your word and looking out for my girl. I really do appreciate everything, and I know she does too."

Cena shot me a quick smile. "It's not a problem." Our budding conversation seemed to fizzle off until she spoke up again naturally. "So, do you, like, wanna continue to sit and chat for a bit longer, or do you want to get right down to why we're here?" she quizzed.

I shrugged. "Let's just... do it. Let's rip the Band-Aid off," I said, pulling my phone back out.

"Okay, then." Cena agreed while flipping her phone over on the table.

"You got the email pulled up?" I asked her.

"Yeah."

"Alright, let's open it on three. One... two..."

"Three..." We clicked the emails, and my eyes darted from left to right. "Oh shit," Cena blurted out before I had the chance to.

My eyes drifted up to hers. The truth was there in black and white. With a probability of over 99.99999 percent, we *were* sisters. "Shit is right," I responded while reaching out for the glass of water in front of me.

"How do you feel now that you know?"

I gulped down half the glass before coming up for air long enough to answer her. "I don't know… I guess it's kind of surreal."

"Yeah, for sure. Now that we know, where do we go from here?"

I tipped my chin forward in a nod. "Yeah, exactly."

"Is it weird that I want to try to get to know you? I mean, I know what it's like to grow up a twin but not a twin sister. But, I understand if that's of no interest to you, considering."

I knew she was talking about Kas without having to say his name, but I'd managed to get over all of that. "No. I don't think it's weird to want to get to know me. I know this situation is… uncanny, but it's our real life. I think we owe it to ourselves to learn about each other on our terms."

Cena smiled before jolting forward. "Oh shit! I almost forgot I have to get to an important appointment! I'm going to be late if I don't leave soon. Damn this pregnancy brain!" she whined while smacking her palm against her forehead. "I'm so sorry!"

I shook my head. "No, it's cool. It's totally fine."

"But I have your number, okay? So, we'll, like, find time to do lunch and hang out."

"That sounds nice."

"I'll see you later," she said while slowly getting up from the table and waddling away.

I waved. "Bye."

* * *

I ARRIVED BACK at my apartment to find a large black box leaning against the door with a notecard tucked behind the oversized bow.

"What the hell is this?" I mumbled while moving it to the side to unlock the door.

I set my keys on the counter before returning to pick up the box and bring it inside. After kicking the door closed, I set the box down and opened the notecard.

A car will arrive to pick you up at six. Open the box and wear what's inside. -Kas

I set the card down before shimmying the bow down the box and removing the lid. Inside was a silver gown decorated with what looked to be thousands of hand-sewn crystals. My eyes popped wide as I pulled it out to give it a deeper inspection. It was a floor-length, mermaid-style gown with a plunging sweetheart neckline and a split that I knew would expose every square inch of my right thigh. I was dying to try it on but decided to text him first and then take a shower.

Me: *The dress is beautiful. What's the occasion?*
Kas: *You'll see.*
Me: *Not even a hint?*
Kas: *I'll see you later, Jrue.*

I kissed my teeth before entering my bedroom to drape the gown across my bed. His secrecy was getting on my nerves, but I wasn't about to pick a fight. Whatever the occasion was, I knew it was special. He was being romantic, and I would let him thoroughly sweep me off my feet. After I stepped out of the shower and moisturized my body and curls, I slid on the dress. From how it hugged my curves just right to how the crystals shimmered in the light, you would've thought he'd gotten it custom-made. I called him with a broad smile splashed across my face.

"I thought I told you I'd see you later," he answered.

"I know. I just wanted to say thank you. I tried it on, and it fits like a glove," I confirmed while admiring my reflection.

"You can thank me in person."

"You're on your way to pick me up?"

"No, but your car will be arriving soon."

I frowned. "Wait. You're not picking me up yourself?"

"The car I sent will bring you to me."

"And exactly where are you?"

"I'll see you soon, Jrue," he said before ending the call.

I smacked my teeth before sliding my silver heels on my feet and grabbing my purse. A couple of minutes later, my phone rang with a call from a number I didn't recognize.

"H-hello?"

"Ms. Norwood?" a man with a heavy Latin accent inquired.

"Who is this?"

"Hello, ma'am. I'm Miguel, your driver. I am calling to tell you I am downstairs waiting for you at your building's entrance."

My tone softened. "Oh, um, okay. Thank you. I'll be right down."

I stepped outside to see a man holding open the door to a black Mercedes-Maybach S-Class and almost lost my balance. "What in the hell is this man up to?" I whispered before getting inside.

After a silent twenty-minute drive, Miguel finally spoke. "We are here, ma'am."

The car came to a slow stop as I turned my attention out of the window and saw that we were near a marina.

"Where exactly is *here*?" I questioned with confusion laced in my tone.

"Let me show you."

Miguel got out of the car and came around to open my door before extending his hand to help me out.

"Now, where am I supposed to be going?"

"There," he said while extending his finger to one of the many yachts aligning the water's edge. "I will escort you, ma'am."

"Okay, then. Let's go."

I took hold of his arm as we slowly descended the concrete walkway that followed the waterway. The gentle waves crashed against the rocks at the marina as the cloud-filled sky burst with hot pink and lavender hues. The closer we got to the sixty-foot snow-white yacht, the more my nerves began to bounce around in my stomach.

I pulled in a deep breath as the cool ocean breeze brushed against my skin. "Whose yacht is this?" I asked Miguel, but he kept his eyes forward.

He slowly escorted me out onto the old wooden dock that stretched out onto the water and then across the ladder-like walkway onto the luxury boat's entrance.

"This is as far as I go, ma'am," he disclosed before turning away.

I looked up to see the stairs lined with rose petals and a different person standing on each step. A violinist was performing his rendition of Case's "Happily Ever After." There was another with both arms filled with dozens and dozens of long-stem red roses. Others had snapped open jewelry boxes filled with sparkling necklaces, watches, and bracelets. And standing at the top of the stairs was Kas.

"You look more beautiful than I imagined you would look in that dress." He complimented me.

I looked up at him and smiled. "See, I told you it fits like a glove."

"That's what custom-made feels like."

My brows lurched up my forehead. "Wait. What? Custom? How'd you even know what size?"

"You left your clothes at my house a couple of weeks ago, remember?"

"Wow. You are too slick for words."

"Is that a good thing or a bad thing?" he inquired, taking me into his arms and kissing my cheek.

"Ask me later. Right now, I want to know what all of this is, and what's the occasion?"

"*You* are the occasion, Jrue. Today. Tomorrow. Always. I want to give you the world. Everything you deserve."

I reached up to gently caress the side of his face. "All I need is you."

"And as of this afternoon, you *officially* have all of me."

My gaze found his. "What?"

"We dissolved our marriage today, Jrue. Cena and I are done."

His confirmation made my heart skip a beat. "So, it's official, huh? That's it?"

Kas nodded. "That's it. We signed the papers with the lawyer earlier today. No strings. No stipulations."

I cleared my throat as emotion stirred behind my eyes. "Well, how's it feel to be a single man again?"

Kas looked at me with sincerity written in his eyes. "Ain't shit about me single, Jrue. I'm *your* man. Now, come on. Have a glass of champagne with me."

He took my hand in his before escorting me to a private space he'd carved out for the two of us on board the yacht. The orange glow of flickering candles traced the perimeter of a heart made of rose petals. Fairy lights were draped across the railing to cast a romantic glow as the sun's hue began to dim from a bright, lemony yellow to a sky full of gold before submerging behind us.

"This is too beautiful, Kas."

"I'm glad you like it."

"I *love* it," I corrected him.

"I had to come correct for you," he said before walking over to retrieve the expensive bottle of champagne chilling in the bucket and popping it open. Kas poured into my glass until the bubbles crowned the rim and spilled over the sides.

"What are we toasting to?" I asked before raising my glass.

"Our forever."

My teeth flashed white and broad. "I like the sound of that."

We clinked our glasses together before he approached me from behind and took me in his arms. My eyes panned the landscape while cradled in his grasp. The buildings near the dock had all become distant silhouettes. I'd been so swept up in Kas that I hadn't noticed we'd been moving. We'd gone from shore to suddenly surrounded by nothing but water and completely isolated from the outside world. I closed my eyes and let the enchanting sounds of the boat skipping against the waves calm me.

"I meant what I said about our forever. It starts here, Jrue. Tonight," he said.

I twisted my neck to look at him. "I know you said your marriage is over, but what about your family?"

"I don't give a fuck about what my father or anyone else has to say. I'm done with The Order. I'm done with everything, especially when it comes to my inability to live on my fuckin' terms. Kamil can take over for me if he has to. You've got my heart, woman. I don't give a fuck about anything or no one else but you."

"So what are you saying?"

"I'm saying, there ain't no way I'm fuckin' lettin' you go again," he said before getting down on one knee.

I stepped back before cupping my hands over my mouth to cover my gasp. "Oh! My God! Oh my God! Oh my! My God!" I blubbered as tears sprang out of my eyes.

He took my trembling hand in his. "Before you, the thought of getting married never even crossed my mind. Then when I found out I couldn't have you in my life the way that I wanted to, I knew I couldn't let that shit go; that I had to make it right because I'm too in love with you to let you walk out of my life for good," he confessed before dipping into his pocket and pulling out a red velvet ring box.

He popped it open, and I felt my knees go weak. "Oh my God, Kas."

"Say yes, Jrue. Tell me that you love me, too, and that you'll be my wife."

"Yes! I love you. Yes! I love you so much, Kas. Yes! A million fuckin' times, yes!" I squealed before he slipped the ring onto my finger.

Kas crashed his body against mine before spinning me around in the air. I glanced down at the dazzling rock on my finger with a smile that could never be erased. I was ready to spend the rest of my life as Mrs. Kasim Barnes.

Twenty-Four

JRUE

Seven months later
Los Cabos, Mexico

HAPPINESS FLICKERED in my eyes as I sat at the vanity, staring at my reflection. Everything was perfect, from my white, mermaid-style wedding gown with hand-sewn crystals and beading from head to toe, to the soft, romantic curls cascading down my open back. Tears burned the back of my throat as I sat back and replayed every smile, every tear, and every heartbreak we'd endured since the moment we met. Everything it took to get to this moment. Had it all been worth it? Would I do it all over again? My answer was yes.

"You look beautiful, Jrue," my mother complimented, snapping me out of my thought bubble.

I shot a face-splitting grin at her through her reflection in the mirror. "Thanks."

"You almost ready?"

"Yeah. I am," I paused. "It means a lot that you're here with me today, Mama."

"There's no place else I'd rather be."

I placed my hands on her shoulders and looked into her eyes. "You know that no matter who physically brought me into this world, *you* are my mother. You are my *only* mother," I assured her.

Tears burned the borders of her eyes. "Thank you, baby. You were the best decision I ever made, and it's an honor to be your mother. Now, enough with all of that. Are you ready for this?" my mother asked me.

I laced my arm in hers. "I am."

"Then let's get you down to the beach and get you a husband!"

The live saxophonist began his rendition of "Whenever Wherever Whatever" by Maxwell, and everyone rose from their seats. Arm in arm, my mother and I inched down the aisle with scattered white rose petals, slowly placing one foot in front of the other. I looked up, and my breath hitched. Kasim Barnes was standing at the end of that aisle wearing the *hell* out of a white Hugo Boss tuxedo, black velvet loafers, and a pair of black Louis Vuitton sunglasses. With each step, I kept my eyes trained on him, the depths of my gaze bottomless as I clutched my cascading bouquet filled with bright white roses, orchids, and greenery.

The calm waves crashed against the sand a few feet from our beach ceremony. I adjusted my view away from him, only to exchange a brief smile with Charity and Yara, holding her baby girl. Although we opted not to have bridesmaids or groomsmen, I was happy to have the people closest to us in attendance, including his brother Kamil and his wife Janessa, Cena, Liam, and their son.

Moisture spilled through my lashes as I took his hand in mine. We made our way up to the arch overflowing with white flowers, greenery, and soft candlelight. Everything felt draped in love and romance.

Joy clouded his eyes as he leaned in to kiss my cheek. "Hey, you," he whispered in my ear.

I managed to pass him a soft smile through my trembling lids. "Hi."

Tears of joy skipped down my cheeks as I pulled in a deep breath through my nose and pushed it out through my lips. Before Kas, I had every reason not to believe in love. Never in a million years did I expect to be standing next to him, ready to spend the rest of my life tethered to him. And yet, I wouldn't have had it any other way. I was convinced our souls hadn't met by accident. Kas knew me inside and out, chapter and verse. We exchanged rings and vows before the officiant announced us.

Kas placed his soft, juicy lips against mine as his fingertips gently grazed the sides of my face. We'd officially started our new chapter as husband and wife, just the two of us against the world. Somewhere beyond right and wrong, we'd found our happily ever after. This time, *love won.*

The End

Afterword

A note from K.L. Hall.

Reader,

Thank you for reading the finale of *Crushed Velvet & Cashmere*. If you've made it this far, I hope you'll consider taking a minute to tell me what you thought about the book in the form of a **review and/or rating**. Don't hesitate to let me know what you'd like to see from me next! I thoroughly enjoy reading your thoughts and hearing from you as well! I'm always striving to attract new and retain current readers, and reviews are one of the easiest ways to attract readers. Tell a friend if you loved the book, and most importantly, let me know!

All my love,

K.L. Hall

About the Author

K.L. Hall is a national bestselling and award-winning author. As a serial storyteller, Hall has penned over three dozen titles in various genres—including African American urban fiction and romance, paranormal, children's books (as Kimberley M.), and non-fiction. Her fictional stories straddle the intersection of classic Urban and spell-binding Romance.

Highly Acclaimed Titles:

In the Arms of a Savage: (Peaked at #1 in Women's Fiction)

The Potomac Falls Series (Peaked at #1 and #2 in African American Erotica)

Sign up for my mailing list to stay updated with new releases, giveaways, sneak peeks, and more! Click this link: https://bit.ly/38RMpV5 *(E-Book Only)*

Connect with me on social media:

Facebook: https://www.facebook.com/authorklhall

Twitter: https://twitter.com/authorklhall

Instagram: https://www.instagram.com/officialklhall/

Website: https://www.authorklhall.com

Other novels by K.L. Hall:

Diary of a Hood Princess 1-3

Rise of a Street King: The Justice Silva Story *(Spin-Off to the Diary of a Hood Princess series)*

Broken Condoms and Promises 1-3

In the Arms of a Savage 1-3

Built for a Savage: Blaze and Camille's Love Story *(Spin-Off to the In the Arms of a Savage Series)*

A Ruthle$$ Love Story 1-3

Fallin' for the Alpha of the Streets 1-2

The Most Savage of Them All: The Wolfe Calloway Story *(Prequel to the In the Arms of a Savage Series)*

When a Gangsta Loves a Good Girl

Caught Between my Husband and a Hustler

The Illest Taboo 1-2

To the Only Thug I'll Ever Love

A Lover's Heist: Chief and Gianna's Love Story

A Lover's Heist II: Rome and Lira's Love Story

A Lover's Heist III: Baby and Skai's Love Story

Crushed Velvet & Cashmere

Crushed Velvet & Cashmere 2

Short Reads + Novellas:

Bi-Curious: An Erotic Tale

Bi-Curious 2: Tastes Like Candy

House of Cards 1-2

A Savage Calloway Christmas *(Christmas novella to the In the Arms of a Savage Series)*

Lovin' the Alpha of the Streets: A Valentine's Day Novella *(Valentine's Day novella to the Fallin' for the Alpha of the Streets Series)*

Awakened: A Paranormal Romance

As Long as You Stay Down

Solace in Seven

Solace II: The Final Cut

Something Bleu

Something Borrowed

Something New

The Knight Before Christmas: A Potomac Falls Short

I'll Be Home for Christmas: A Potomac Falls Short Book II

Children's Books:

Princess for Hire
Princess Twinkle Toes & the Missing Magic Sneakers
Little One, Change the World
Adjust Your Crown: A Self-Love Coloring Book for Children of Color

Non-Fiction:
Authors are a Business: The Booked & Busy Course Mini Book

Thank You

Thanks for reading! If you enjoyed this book, please leave a review on Amazon and mark it as read on Goodreads. We hate errors but they do happen. If you catch any, please send them to us directly at blovepublications@gmail.com with ERRORS as the subject.

www.ingramcontent.com/pod-product-compliance
Lightning Source LLC
La Vergne TN
LVHW010550160826
845677LV00013B/3069